Festive Fugitive

Murder & Mistletoe Anthology Series

K.A. Merikan

Cover design by

MiblArt

https://miblart.com/

Editing by No Stone Unturned

https://www.facebook.com/NoStoneUnturnedEditingServices/

Contents

CHAPTER 1

CESAR

YOU KNOW HOW THEY say to not gift a puppy for Christmas? This rule should be extended to not giving away your child to erase a gambling debt, but my parents already did that, so I don't get a vote.

At thirty-three, I've had a lifetime to resent the Holiday season, but this year is especially aggravating. This year was supposed to be the Christmas when I get my freedom back from the man who took me in, trained me, tortured me, and made me his favorite weapon.

The man who's been refusing to take my calls and left my messages on 'read', communicating through an assistant who can never give me any information. I've killed, maimed, and bled for him, but since I lost my eye, I've only been given menial jobs that don't make full use of my skills, nor are worthy of praise.

At first, I thought it was because I lost some muscle mass during the rehabilitation period, but I've been determined in my training, and I know I'm ready to buy my life out with a final deed. If only Sullivan lets me.

That is why I am here, enduring the greens, reds, and golds, the cheerful music that reminds me of the last time I saw my mother. The air smells of pine, but it's an artificial aroma originating from diffusers, and the undertone of fakeness it carries makes the protein bar I've eaten rise in my throat. My artificial eye feels particularly alien in its socket tonight. I haven't worn it for days, but Sullivan doesn't like it when I walk around with an eyepatch, so I bear with the discomfort for the sake of putting him in a good mood.

Sullivan loves to show off, so he paid for this grand gala to celebrate him becoming the new mayor. As his bodyguard—my replacement—trails behind him, I can see the mistakes he's making from my spot on the mezzanine. To think I was tossed aside in favor of such a rookie... If Sullivan had more brains than cruelty in him, he'd have at least three guys like Lyle guarding him. This asshole was far too busy glancing at a woman in a short red dress to spot the man passing far too close to Sullivan. She smells of expensive perfume I can sense all the way up here. Women are not the kind of prey I seek, but the click of heels she makes with every step? As enjoyable as the ticking of a well-timed bomb.

My job tonight is being on standby, which pretty much means doing nothing but remaining on call. I've had enough of that and I *will* talk to my boss. Face-to-face. I might have been a five-year-old sniveling kid when he took me in, but now I'm taller than him, bigger than him, meaner than him, and I could snap his neck if only—

Sullivan and Lyle disappear from my sight, so I move along to see them descend the stairs. They're headed for the restrooms. Perfect.

Whatever happens, I *will* convince him to set me free, to let me enjoy a future I've been preparing for years now. It's the least I deserve after everything I've sacrificed for him. I might not know the exact debt my parents accumulated, but my work must have long paid it off. With interest.

I will *not* be ignored.

I push my way through a sea of guests and staff, including the waiters in Santa outfits. I'd call the way silver beards cover their faces a security risk, but I guess it's not my job anymore. I snarl at someone who pops a cracker filled with glitter right next to me, covering the whole arm of my black suit in shiny particles.

Someone's camera flashes close by, and I stiffen as the hair on my nape bristles. For a terrible moment, I expect lightning to go through my body, but we're indoors, the weather outside is as perfect as it can be in December, and I have no reason to fear a storm tonight, so I ball my hands into fists and offer the guy with the cracker a fake smile. My boss would resent me if I slit this bastard's throat, but I wish I could do it anyway. At least it's just my glorified uniform, not something I wear because I want to.

When I can, my style of choice is much more utilitarian. A soft hoodie, a fitted T-shirt, a bomber jacket allowing movement, and cargo pants with many pockets to hide weapons, paired with combat boots to crush people's toes with ease.

I have to accept the civilian's apology, because I don't want to lose Sullivan in favor of an argument I don't truly care about. Shiny tinsel hangs over the restroom doors, as if pissing in December was somehow different from doing it any other time of the year.

When both men disappear inside, I stand with my back to the door and listen. I know Sullivan well enough to realize I shouldn't give him too much time to think things through, so I only enter once I hear the splash of water. The two pairs of eyes stab my chest, but I ignore the sharpness of their gazes, remaining calm even when Lyle's hand gravitates to the gun holstered at his side. Nothing good would come from a scuffle right now.

A part of me is pleased when Sullivan stiffens. It means that no matter how long he's been ignoring me, he sees me as dangerous. Worth a degree of respect. So I give him a curt nod.

"Why are you here, Cesar?" he asks, shaking water off his hands. "You were meant to be on standby tonight."

Like any other day in recent times. It did give me plenty of reading time, but each passing week feels like confirmation that I'm no longer needed, and that Sullivan wants to punish me for getting injured in the first place. As if I haven't taken that stab in the eye for him.

A part of me knows his life should not be more important than my own health, but like every well-trained dog in existence, I can't resist the compulsion to fight for my master.

"May I have a word, sir?" I ask, hoping Lyle takes the hint and leaves the two of us alone, but he remains in the restroom, watching me as if I'm an outsider.

Sullivan exhales, making me feel like even more of a burden. "It's fine, Lyle, you can leave us, just stay outside and don't let anyone in. This won't take long."

Another slap in the face.

Lyle gives me a dirty look I couldn't give less of a shit about, and I'm finally alone with the man who pretty much owns me. I should hate him, and sometimes disdain weaves its way into my heart, but it never stays long. He's the closest thing to a parent I've ever had. It's because of him that I have a life, plenty of money in my bank account, and the possibility of a future.

"So? What is it, Cesar?"

I clear my throat, ready to recite the few sentences I've memorized over the past few days. But when my mouth opens, it's as if something's wiped my memory clean. With sweaty hands, I nod, struggling to speak, even though I know exactly what I came here to say.

I'm a grown man. A pot-bellied seventy-year old with skin sunburned after his most recent skiing trip shouldn't make me so flustered, and yet here I am, embarrassed like a child who's broken his parents' antique vase. He's shorter than me, weaker, but something inside me still sees him as the towering figure who greeted me at his home so many years ago.

"I—I wanted to speak to you, sir. It's been a long time, and another year's gone by. I understand I'm not owed anything for the previous one, because of my injury, but I was active and ready in the past twelve months. I'd like to ask if you picked my tattoo yet."

The last one, and we both know it. The only Christmas presents I ever got, etched into my skin from the year of my first kill at fifteen.

"And do you feel you've earned one this year, Cesar?"

It's so condescending I want to grab his gray head and smash it into the sink, sending teeth and brains flying into every corner of this restroom. How's that for Christmas decorations?

But I won't. The power this man holds over me is greater than the strength of his muscles could ever be. I won't be free of him until he takes off my leash.

"I'm ready each day with the exception of Fridays. My loyalty is flawless," I say without thinking, because it is not my fault he chooses not to use me for any job of note.

"My Dobermans don't need days off." He chuckles, but his eyes remain cold. He's comparing me to dogs. Is it a slight? Or is he telling me to do better? Despite the compulsion to keep him happy, I won't give up on the one evening when I can roam free and bury myself in handsome bodies, so I stay silent. "The holidays are a busy time. I will see about it in the new year."

Bile rises in my throat. That means another year in his service. Twelve more months of wasted time. Have I not done enough? Don't I deserve to finally start living for myself and breathe air rather than the smoke of my master's cigars? I've got this planned out. A house off the Alaskan coast, freedom to see people or not. I could fuck someone every day if I felt like it, and even hunt, if my instincts need to be sated.

"What are you keeping me for, if you don't plan to use me? Give me a job worthy of that tattoo, and I'll do it before the year's over." I look straight into his eyes, something I was taught not to do, and step closer to show him how much bigger I am.

Sullivan stills, but I notice the single drop of sweat beading on his temple.

Yes, motherfucker. You nurtured a beast, now deal with it.

He straightens as if that can make him much taller. "I will give you a job when I choose to. You don't call the shots here. Or should I use *the words* to remind you? Unless you actually want to kill me and test whether the implant in your heart is real or not?"

I step back as if he's tazed me with a cattle prod, eyes back on the floor.

I hate myself for being like this, but I don't want to risk my life, or have him ever use *the words* on me again. I shake my head, mouth dry as I move until my back hits the wall.

"No. Of course not. But I want to be useful. I want to be active."

I don't dare look up, but I can *sense* his gaze. Full of disdain.

"I will find something worthy of your talents in due time," Sullivan says coolly.

It's a compliment. A pat on the back after a slap, but it doesn't cheer me up. He means to keep me for another year. Maybe he wants me to die on the job, so there's no loose ends.

I don't get to answer. He walks past me and exits the restroom, leaving me with the ghost of his peppery scent.

For several heartbeats, I remain still, my gaze pinned to the sealant between floor tiles, but then I'm at the sink and dunk my face under the faucet. Icy water splashes the back of my head, forming rivulets through my hair. There's so much anger in me, but not being able to express it makes me numb.

Will this always be my life?

I walk out as if on autopilot, then find my way back up the stairs and to the mezzanine where I'm *on standby*. Like an outdated gaming console you're not using anymore, but *maybe* you'll want to pick up the joystick at some point, so why not just keep it indefinitely?

Since I'm not required to do much, I let my gaze follow a man in a sharp burgundy suit. Slim, with a neat haircut and pretty lips, he glances my way as well, and I consider an act of rebellion against Sullivan's rules. It's not Friday, but maybe I could sneak away with this stranger and fuck his brains out to forget tonight's disastrous meeting. I might appear silly with wet hair and water dripping onto my glitter-infested suit, but couldn't that serve as an easy conversation starter?

Some animals bond for life, but my heart isn't capable of love, so I make do with lust, taking whatever I need for the brief moments I get to hold someone in my arms.

I look straight into the man's eyes—something I enjoy doing a little too much. Probably because I'm not allowed to be so direct with Sullivan.

But then a gunshot resonates through the room, the stranger screams and crouches, but I, like Pavlov's dog, turn back toward the danger to find Sullivan in the crowd below.

He stumbles into Lyle's arms, knocking him over while guests crouch, shrieking so loudly I can barely hear the second shot.

A bloom of red spreads over Sullivan's white shirt, and I can't believe what I'm seeing.

The shooter is wearing a Santa costume. He's just feet away from Sullivan, his trembling hand still extended with the gun in it as people shriek and run, tripping over each other.

Impossible.

This amateur stands there, looking around as if he can't believe what he's done. As if he has no escape plan. I catch a glimpse of his eyes and pull out my gun. I have a clear shot. I could take him out and put an end to this now.

It's a split-second decision, yet my whole life manages to flash through my mind. All the pain Sullivan caused me, who I've become because of him, the invisible collar I'm wearing.

This stranger shot through the links of my chain with two bullets.

He doesn't deserve a shot in the forehead. He deserves my gratitude and protection, because otherwise, he's not getting out of here alive.

When, painful seconds later, he finally flees, I lower my gun and run to follow.

CHAPTER 2

ELI

I'VE NEVER SHOT ANYONE before. The gun in my hand and the odor of burnt gunpowder feel so out of place. I'm having a full-on out-of-body experience and I see myself in this horrifying, yet ridiculous scene.

I'm at a Christmas gala, dressed as Santa, to match the other waiters. In front of me stands Arthur Sullivan, the man who ruined my life, a scumbag mobster who just got elected as mayor. I must have lost my mind at the injustice of it. I brought my gun to threaten him in some secluded corner, say my piece to him, and... I don't even know what.

But then I got close, saw the opportunity, and made the split-second decision.

Now, here we are.

My bullets skewer into his chest, and for a second, I'm frozen like the expensive ice sculptures on the tables.

All it takes is the screams erupting for me to turn around despite my brain being as empty as a bauble.

What a fuck up.

What have I done?

Sullivan deserved it, but did I ruin what's left of my sorry life? I'm only twenty-five.

Is... everything over for me?

I suppose it's not like I have anywhere to go to enjoy Christmas this year. Might as well spend the festive season in jail. *Har-har.*

Guests flee. Others duck under the large tables, but it's all a blur. The only sharp point ahead is a corridor I can use as my quickest way out of here, as if my lizard brain activated to increase the chance of survival.

Fat fucking chance.

A security officer darts my way like a quarterback speeding for the touchdown. I might be tall, but months of undereating means I'm skinny as fuck. If that bulldozer gets his hands on me, I'm done. But just as he's about to clash with me, I hear a gunshot, and he falls on his face with a sickening crack.

Who made that shot?

Tumbling past me, the officer slaps my shin with his arm, and that jerks me out of my stupor.

The speakers still blast 'Jingle Bells' when I set off past a row of Christmas trees with decorations referencing various countries of the world. A table crowded with soft drinks is in my way, but it can't hold me back. Plastic bottles, cups, and jugs collapse like bowling pins, but just as I reach the other end, damp but whole, a gang of elves descends on me out of nowhere.

I swear that in the corner of my eye I see another Santa being tackled, so at least my disguise is of some use, even if the red stands out like Rudolph's nose.

I make an instant turn when the men in green costumes close in on me. It would have been a hilarious scene if I hadn't shot Arthur Sullivan point-blank.

A tower of gift boxes, as tall as a Christmas tree, becomes my target. When I slam into it, some of them fall on me, but most topple behind me. The elves fall over like characters in some gruesome sequel to *Home Alone*. In my case, it would be called *Homeless Alone*.

The elves are yelling something, one even manages to jump over the mound of presents, but I turn my gun at him while running, and he falls to the ground. I don't intend to shoot anyone else, but I'll do what I can to get to my car.

I have no illusions about what's to happen next.

I've fucked up big time.

I've fucked up so bad, I might as well consider my life over.

But even though it might be for the best if I give myself up now, something inside prompts me to try the impossible and run.

There will be a manhunt, with helicopters, trained dogs, and hundreds of cops, and I can't see freedom in my future, but some tiny voice at the back of my head whispers that there's always a chance. Camping out in the deep, deep woods no one ever goes to. Or, somehow evading capture and settling in a country with no extradition treaty with the US. For that, I'll need way more money than my meager belongings are worth, but there's no point counting my chickens before they're hatched.

All I know now is I need to keep moving. To change my appearance and disappear.

Inflatables depicting festive creatures stare at me, jeering as I dash past them, bursting through the door only used by staff, then down the hallway, straight for the exit.

I don't know how, but I've managed to lose my pursuers. Even the exit sign above the door seems to be winking at me with its wonky light.

For the split second when I slam into the door, I expect it to be locked, but no, I burst into the cold air outside, and not a soul awaits me here. No cops yet, only the twinkling lights on a row of giant Christmas trees.

I sprint through the dark parking lot like a madman and reach my car in record time. I didn't even know I could run this fast. I rip my beard off on the way, and my jacket is already open when I get to my belongings in the back seat. I did plan for an escape, so I'm fully dressed under the Santa outfit. All I need to do in order to not appear immediately suspicious is take it off, and put on a jacket.

I change faster than Superman in a telephone booth, and I'm behind the wheel of my junk ride in no time, high on adrenaline.

I release the handbrake, then shove the keys into the ignition, turn and— nothing happens.

It's as if I'd been stabbed with a hot poker, but when I try again, and then for the third time, my vehicle chokes, trembles... and stays dead.

This isn't the first time this has happened—it's a very old car, and the December cold isn't playing in my favor either, but I wasn't too worried about the unreliability of my ride when I parked earlier. Mostly because I never intended to pull the trigger, and the worst I expected was a fine for disturbing the peace.

That ship has sailed.

Maybe I should have chosen a car based on reliability, not how much space it has inside, but that wasn't really an option when it has to accommodate all the shit I own.

Now, my only choice is to leave it all behind.

My car will be found, and my identity discovered along with it.

With a lump in my throat, I open the car door as I think of all the bad choices I've made in my life. And yet, I can't regret my actions. Sullivan got what he deserved even if I'll pay for revenge with my life.

My heart sinks when I spot several police cars driving into the parking lot with a squeak of wheels. They stop right by the tall Christmas trees, their headlights on me as cops flood out of the vehicles, yelling something I can't hear with the thudding in my head.

They're about to get me, I'm sure of it, but just as I'm on the verge of lifting my hands in defeat, the largest of the trees tips over, descending onto the vehicles like a whale crashing onto a boat in the middle of the ocean. The cops scatter, for a moment forgetting my existence in favor of saving their lives, and this is my chance.

Unbelievably, I still have one.

I'm about to shoot across the parking lot, out of sight, when I spot someone retreating into the shadows of the building, very close to the base of the collapsed tree. I swear it's a real man, not some phantom my mind has created in its panicked state. I might be a fool, but not enough to squander a chance when it's thrown at me, so I dash past the steel barrier at the edge of the lot and tumble down a hill, beyond the glow of the streetlights.

Thank fuck I don't hear dogs.

Christmas miracle?

CHAPTER 3

CESAR

HE'S TOO THIN. NOT that he's unattractive. But if it were up to me, I'd put him on a regimen of nutritionally-dense foods, with plenty of protein, broth for collagen, and lots of fresh vegetables, to help with whatever deficiencies he must surely be dealing with. I've shadowed him for the past twenty-four hours and know he hasn't had a single bite of food in that time.

At this rate, he might collapse from hunger and exhaustion, but even then he would be in no danger. Not on my watch.

The cops must have gotten his name based on the registration of the abandoned car. It's Elijah, but he goes by Eli on social media, so that's how I choose to think about him as I watch his shoulders from the back of the bus. Most people won't be able to recognize him from the old photo publicized all over the media. Since it was taken, his features have sharpened, giving his already narrow face a fox-like appearance. And most importantly, there's no brown left on his head, just a mix of dark and bright grays. It's unusual on a man as young as him. Silver dusted over dark steel. A bold choice. Most men his age would have cropped it shorter to not bring attention to it, but he's grown it into a wavy mop that reaches past his ears. Then again, maybe he just can't afford a barber. The padded jacket he's wearing is two sizes too big and mended in at least three places. Worst are the shoes, with one of the soles opening like a mouth when he walks.

But now that I've memorized his scent, I could follow him anywhere, even if he managed to disguise his appearance. He doused himself in some cheap orange and cinnamon perfume he picked up from a street seller, but as unpleasant as the intensity of that aroma is, the natural musk of Eli's body is shining through the more the deodorant wears off. I can't quite put my finger on it yet, but as I trail him, checking out places he touched, the scent of sand or... dust is quite prominent, as well as a hint of natural sweetness, which I long to taste straight from the source.

That's not why I'm following him, of course, and Eli's likely as interested in men as the vast majority of the male population, but I am free in my fantasies and imagine myself on top of his slender form, face buried between his shoulder-blades, and dick getting warm in his crack.

I spread my legs to take pressure off my half-hard cock and try to think of something else, because this is not the right time for pleasure.

Eli doesn't seem to have anywhere to go, and I've been shadowing him since yesterday. It's a miracle no one's recognized him yet, but if that happens, I'll be there to protect him, like I already did during that first dash from the murder scene. It's the least I can do for someone who put an end to my service.

It's regretful I didn't get to be at Arthur Sullivan's side when he died. The smell of his blood would have been rich with adrenaline and cortisol, but I've seen it happen, and that's all the closure I require. I'm no longer on his leash, but after years with the invisible chain around my neck, I can't help but feel attached to the one who freed me. Especially when he's so in need of my help.

Running out of the gala, he was like a drunken rabbit pursued by a pack of proficient hounds. He would have ended up torn apart if it wasn't for my intervention with the giant tree. When you save someone's life, it's a special kind of bond that develops. You've invested. You can't let go.

I don't know what to do about this sudden new attachment, but I am adrift without Sullivan, so I might as well go with it for now, admiring the frail, inexperienced killer who accomplished what I wasn't able to despite my background as an assassin, bodyguard, and even torturer. Whatever Sullivan commanded, I did.

When the bus stops and Eli gets up, I do the same, lured by the aroma of his flesh. He needs gloves. His fingers are so slim and pale I can just about imagine their touch. I'd suck on each one with pleasure and warm them in my mouth. It's not what I'm following him for, but I'm not one to push away intrusive thoughts when they're of the tasty variety.

I'm not sure where he thinks he's headed, but we've stopped in Nowhere, Oregon, and he's been traveling north, so he might be hoping for an escape to Canada. In those shoes, he won't make it without losing toes.

His hood is up when he walks fast down the street decorated with Christmas lights. It hides his steel-gray hair which is the perfect length for grabbing. Maybe he has some kind of accomplice in this town? I'll find out sooner or later.

Instead of heading straight for whatever place he might have in mind, Eli stops in front of a bright shop window, and the television screen reflects its colors onto his pale face. His profile's sharp, with a large yet narrow nose, and uneven lips. The top one is larger, and rather chewable. Mouths like that are addictive, and I know I'd get hooked if I ever got the chance for a taste.

As I drift closer, attempting to be one with the shadows, the reason for his interest becomes obvious. If he has any sense, he'll have already discarded his phone, and it's only now that he gets to catch a glimpse of the shit he's in.

The cops have long identified him, scoured through all the evidence in his car, concluding the killer's homeless, twenty-five, and the media even came up with a catchy name for Eli, dubbing him the 'Festive Fugitive'.

I watch him stiffen, then blow warm air on those pale hands. I wouldn't mind if he wanted to slide them under my sweater for warmth. But the moment the screen goes on to show a portrait of Sullivan, Eli walks off, his wrecked shoe slapping loudly with every step. I promised myself I'd watch from afar, make sure no one interferes with his escape. That seems like a reasonable thing to do for a man who ended Sullivan for me.

Only I haven't slept in over twenty-four hours either, so my mind is getting a little too dazed with fantasies of 'what if?'. Eli had a snooze on the bus, but I couldn't allow myself the luxury of rest. He's become my priority as soon as I understood what he'd done, and following him without revealing my presence is a struggle. He's not dressed right for this snowy weather. He doesn't seem to have any escape plans, and here I am, hoping he is not as clueless as he appears. At this rate, he'll make some terrible blunder, and I'll have to save the day.

Then, I'll have to be close to him, tempted by his scent and the shape of his ass. I've seen its outline when he bent over, and if it were Friday and he—a stranger at the sauna, I'd have dived my face between those tempting globes long ago.

I understand what his goal is when I spot a food truck boasting about their seasonal roast turkey sandwiches. I can only hope he buys two, because he could use some protein in him. He should also take a third to go if he's smart.

I wish I knew more about him. It would help me navigate my task of keeping him safe.

Eli passes the empty wooden benches where customers can sit down to eat by the warmth of an outdoor heater and approaches the truck. It's decorated with festive lights, and every twinkle reminds me that I'm stuck without my last Christmas gift from Sullivan. But I'll worry about that once Eli is safe.

I stand back, watching him order his food, and then coffee, and the sight of a bank card makes my blood run quicker. He can't be this ignorant. If he uses that thing, the cops will be here in under five minutes, so I step forward, ready to stop him, but he catches himself on time and stuffs the offending plastic back into his ratty wallet.

With this emergency avoided, I let myself relax, but the single fiver Eli plucks out next won't be enough to cover his meal. He's fiddling with the coin purse under the watchful eye of the truck owner, but both he and I already know Eli doesn't have enough cash on him.

I told myself I wouldn't interact with him, just protect him from afar like a guardian angel. But now I find myself stepping forward, with my own wallet out. "I'll also have the signature turkey sandwich, and a coffee," I say and put a large bill on the money tray. "My treat," I add when Eli turns his big gray eyes to me. They're large, with dark rings around the paler iris, and appear almost iridescent in the glow of the twinkling lights. He's even more hand-some from up close and just my type.

"Are you sure?" he asks from behind the scarf he pulled up high to be less recognizable. "Thank you," he adds without waiting for an answer, because he's desperate to eat. Obviously.

I smile. "Isn't Christmas the time for good deeds?"

He looks at his shoes with a frown, probably imagin-ing his own 'good deed' from yesterday. What was *his* grudge against Sullivan? The police haven't yet leaked much about that. It shouldn't matter, but the closer I am to him, the more I want to find out, and I already crossed the boundary of talking to him.

Even his voice is pleasant to the ear—much lower than I expected, and it has depth and darkness to it, like strong black coffee. It's as addictive already.

Eli takes a deep breath. "I suppose it is. I've had a... rough day, so thanks for this, really. I don't usually need help."

I should let him go. Wait for my food and scurry off to continue watching him from far away, but he glances at me again, curious what I might want, so I clear my throat and shrug. "I want to see you eat. Hope that's not too strange?"

He might be a killer, but is he strong enough to break the social contract after I bought him food? Does he want to? Reasonably, he's a fugitive. He should stay away from people. Especially in a situation that will require him to pull down his scarf. So what will it be?

Eli nods as the seller hands him his food and coffee. When he assesses me, does he like what he sees, or does it not matter to him? Am I someone who bought him food, or is he calculating how much bigger than him I am, in case he needs to fight me off? We're almost the same height, but where I'm a solid wall of muscle under my coat, he's a twig in broken shoes.

"S-sure. I have some time to kill until my bus," he eventually says and leads the way to one of the benches under the colorful lights strung above us.

We take the table closest to the portable heater, and I immediately see the warmth it produces is a huge relief to this young man in threadbare clothes.

He leans a bit closer to me. "Is this like… a fetish thing? You can tell me, I don't judge."

I've only had a pastry and some protein bars since I've started following him, so the savoriness of the sandwich is a blessing. "Do you always go with people's fetishes?" I ask after swallowing the first bite.

He takes a cautious glance around, but then pulls down the scarf to take a bite of his own dinner. His eyes have a sharpness to them, and while his hair is gray, his eyebrows are dark, but his mouth is so pink and sweet I regret he hides it with food so fast.

"Only if they buy me food," he says playfully, meeting my eyes. Does he notice one of them is barely moving? "Sorry, I didn't mean that I do fetish things for food. Let's just rewind all of that, okay?"

He's eating voraciously, as if he's been hungry for much longer than the past twenty-four hours, and I sense a pull of sympathy when I watch him fill his cheeks with the food.

A man who freed me from Sullivan doesn't deserve to be this cold and hungry.

"Do you have a place to sleep? It's cold," I say, to fish if he wouldn't benefit from a motel room somewhere.

He stops chewing and watches me with wide eyes. Fuck, there's nothing particularly special about his features, but I can't stop staring at him. As if I imprinted my loyalty on him the moment he pulled that trigger. "Um... I'm not... I don't... I mean, I'm flattered, but..."

Oh. I guess he's definitely *not* gay?

I lean back, embarrassed when it occurs to me how my offer might have sounded, and I shake my head. "No, nothing like that. It's just that... I know what you did, and I'm on your side. Sullivan deserved it."

There. This was not how I planned this to go, but I need to justify my action *somehow*.

Instead of giving me an answer, he chokes on his food and starts coughing. I was ready to get up if he runs, so I jump to my feet and get to his side of the bench to pat his back.

"Sorry, I shouldn't have blurted it out like that. I'm just still shocked that he's gone," I say, trying to be gentle when I pat him between the shoulder blades. Now that I'm touching him, the jacket seems even thinner, allowing me to sense not only his body heat but also his bony shoulder. He's like the most gorgeous fox, with silver fur and the voice of a wolf. I already imagine trailing my fingers down his prominent spine.

Which I shouldn't, because he's already told me he's not interested.

Eli has some coffee and clears his throat. "Not sure what you mean. I've been mistaken for a lot of people in the past. I just have that face, you know? Kinda forgettable, kinda like everyone and no one," he laughs nervously, speaking all too quickly.

Forgettable? Like fuck. I already have every line of his features memorized. I will never forget his eyes, his silver hair, his fresh, masculine scent. It's been only a day, yet I already know I'd miss him if we part. I've showed my cards, so I might as well make sure he has someplace warm to sleep tonight. It's the least I can do.

"You're fifteen pounds thinner than in your license photo, but I have eyes. Don't worry, the man was scum. I'm on your side." I settle next to him so we can speak quietly, but I do get a bit of a thrill from pressing my thigh against his.

Eli hesitates, but then he meets my eye again. "Sorry I smell like orange cake. I thought it could put the police dogs off my smell. If they were following me that is."

Oh, God. He's even more of a mess than I imagined. But I can deal with that. I can make sure he's safe.

"It is a bit strong. But at least there's no smell of blood, right?" I wink at him.

There's a new darkness in his eyes, as if he's pulled up the curtain and his true feelings are on show. "He did deserve it. I just... I didn't plan it to go that way, I'm no trained killer."

That I know for sure. "You really think I did the right thing?" he asks as if validation from me is the most important thing.

I'm feeling odd, almost as if he's touching my chest, even though both his hands are on the sandwich. Am I just this obsessed with him already, or is my gaydar pinging for good reason? "He deserved to suffer. If it was up to me, he would have bled out torn apart by his own dogs."

Eli's eyes grow wider, but I have to look away. I've always been hypersensitive to sound. That is why I never go to concerts, and sometimes use headphones to block out the noise around me, but the hurried whisper I'm hearing? I don't like it.

My gaze darts to the side as I attempt to locate the source, and my stomach drops when I spot the food truck guy hurriedly ducking back into his kitchen.

To anyone else, this would be nothing, but the puzzle pieces fall together in my head, and while it's possible I'm seeing connections where there are none, caution is the reason I'm still breathing.

"We need to go," I tell Eli and rise from the bench.

He gives me an unsure glance and speaks with his mouth full. "We do?"

A warmth spreads through my chest. He trusts me. He already trusts me to make good decisions for us both despite him being the new man holding *my* leash.

But he's nothing like Sullivan. He deserves to be protected.

"Trust me," I say softly and leave my food behind.

Now I'm regretful I chose to travel on the bus instead of following him in my car.

He isn't looking sure at all, but does get up. He's not letting go of his own sandwich though, as if he's holding it for emotional support. It is a good sandwich, I have to give the food truck owner that. But when I glance at the vendor, I spot him with a phone, glancing our way, then once again disappearing from view.

"Where do we—" Eli starts, but then two cop cars arrive and park nearby without a siren.

They want to seem casual to not spook us, but I've no doubt they're here for Eli.

They're not getting him.

CHAPTER 4

ELI

I'M FUCKED. SO FUCKED.

And yet, this stranger who appears to have a grudge against Sullivan makes me feel like *maybe* something will work out. He oozes confidence in a way that makes me hand over the reins.

He's wearing a black jacket, a thick cowl, combat boots, and he moves like a wolf stalking its prey. His dark hair is slicked back, and when he stands up, shielding me from view, I feel as if the Punisher himself has just become my personal bodyguard.

I'm about to get up and make an exit that doesn't look like fleeing, but he puts a hand on my shoulder. Gently but firmly, he keeps me in place. As if he has a plan.

He told me I should trust him, and while I don't even know his name, I do. I *trust him*.

For a big chunk of my life I had only myself to count on, so I'm used to being the one who makes all the decisions. Him taking over gives me anxiety, but I let him because he seems to know what he's doing, and I don't.

"Keep your face hidden. I'll handle this," the man says, then walks toward the twin vehicles at a pace that can only be called leisurely. Here I am, stiff like a deer in the headlights, and he approaches the cops as if he used to attend the same police academy as them.

"Good evening, officers! This place makes the most amazing sandwiches, doesn't it?" he asks as if this were a fair, not a manhunt.

"Step aside. Now," the cop says, and with no further warning, he pulls out a gun, prompting his buddies to do the same.

My heart sinks, and I can't help but stare back at them, glued to the bench.

Is this how I die? Or will they accept a surrender?

And why did I believe a stranger with confidence in his step would be enough to shield me?

"You should duck," the handsome stranger says. He might be addressing the cops, who seem as baffled as I am, but my body follows the command given in a gravelly voice. A part of me expects pain when a gunshot tears through the air, but it comes with a delay when I take a sudden step back to hide behind the outdoor heater. My foot slips into a hole, my ankle twists under the weight of my body, and a spasm travels up my leg.

I can't stifle a shriek, but the shouting coming from the direction of the cop cars drowns it out. Bullets fly, hitting the truck and even the ground dangerously close to my location, so I keep still despite the agonizing sensation in my ankle. I'd rather be caught than bleed out within the next five minutes. All I can hear is my own heartbeat, and the shriek of a man, followed by a loud *thud*. Then, the same voice that instructed me to hide.

"Show yourself. I know you're back there."

My eyes go wide. What the fuck is happening there that my new protector is still standing? I take a peek from behind the heater, and the scene makes no sense. One of the cops is on the ground, and the other two are cuffed to their car, not making a peep. They're a bit farther from the festive lights above us, so I can't see it all well. Should I... pull out my gun?

"Stay the fuck back!" a man yells from behind the other cop car, so I'm guessing it's the last policeman.

What. The. Fuck?

This is some action movie shit. This does not happen in real life.

But when the radio crackles, and the cop makes an attempt to communicate with someone, my wolf dashes forward and slams his arm down, making everything go quiet.

People are watching us from windows, their focus on the man who's decided to help me for unknown reasons. Despite this being the perfect opportunity to flee, I find myself paralyzed.

Not only because I'm completely out of my comfort zone, but also because he told me to duck. Defying that order now feels like a life and death decision. And how would I even run with my ankle throbbing with more pain by the second?

When this angel of destruction turns back to me and walks with a purpose, I know I won't be moving until he tells me to.

I hear the cocking of a gun right behind me, and for a second, I consider pulling out my own weapon, but it's too late. The guy from the food truck decided to be the hero and points his gun at me.

"Stay still! Both of you!" he yells as if he has authority, but his hands tremble. "On the ground! Not a step closer!"

The dark angel, who's already halfway back to me, exhales, but barely even slows down. "Put the gun on the table."

"Y—you! To the ground," the truck owner rasps in a voice that's likely way weaker than intended. I hold my breath when the stranger walks right into the man's personal space, waiting for the unmistakable bang, and for the burnt scent that always follows. But instead of bleeding out with a bullet in his chest, the man shoves the truck owner's gun aside and slams their foreheads together.

The seller's gun falls to the ground along with him. Dazed, he moans something with his eyes closed, but doesn't attempt to get up.

Black eyes turn to me and I notice something's wrong with one of them. It doesn't move the same as the other. Only by a fraction, but I swear it doesn't. The man seemed perfectly kind when he bought me a sandwich. Now, I see something demonic in him.

And yet I still grab his hand when he urges me to get up. He opens his mouth to talk when we both notice the distant cry of a police siren.

"It couldn't be avoided, I suppose," he mutters, as if the manhunt is a minor inconvenience, then grabs my arm and pulls me along, toward the darkness of a park.

"Let's hurry."

We rush down the street and between the trees. I have to let his arm wrap around my waist because I'm limping, but he smells so good it's hardly a sacrifice on my part. I watch the path under my feet to avoid tripping but keep stealing glances at him in complete shock. "Who... who *are* you?" I choke out. I can't help it, my heart beats ever faster when I notice how handsome his profile is. Or I'm just attracted to how competently he dealt with several people. For me.

"I'll explain. Just not now. I know where to go," he says.

And even though I don't know his name, I follow.

CHAPTER 5

CESAR

I HIGHLY DOUBT THE cops will look for us in a Santa's Grotto on the grounds of the local school. The beauty of small towns is that there are few cameras around, but plenty of unlit alleyways a man can creep through, and police forces are more used to dealing with cattle theft than violent crime.

Sirens keep howling somewhere in the background, but we're safe. For now.

I exhale and watch vapor form in the air.

The dark interior smells of the wood the cabin's made of, and the artificial aroma of pine. There's a fake fireplace on one of the walls, and plenty of decorated boxes piled up behind Eli's tall armchair, but without heating, and laughing children, the grotto is rather depressing.

He's taking off his shoe with a grunt of pain, and I'm eager to find out just how badly he's hurt himself.

"We can only stay here so long. I still didn't get your name. I'm Eli, but you probably already know that," Eli pushes back his hood, revealing the ash and silver hair, and he leans back in the armchair. It feels like he's in a throne, and I, his mere subject, sit on the floor.

"Are you cold?" I ask and remove my cowl before offering it to him. It's the least I can do for the favor he's unknowingly done for me.

Eli cocks his head, watching me as though I'm some curious animal, but takes the scarf. "I've not been warm in a long time. Thank you. I don't think I've even taken in all you've already done for me tonight."

I like his voice. It's masculine, quite low, but there's a softness to it, as if all its edges were wrapped in silk. "Let me look at your ankle?" I ask, shifting closer over the wooden floor, until I'm kneeling at his feet.

I've been forced to my knees in front of Sullivan many times, and this is nothing like that. Eli doesn't threaten me, beat me, or punish me. I'm here because I want to. Because he deserves my help.

"Are you a doctor? You don't look like one." Eli's pale cheeks gain a bit of color when I roll his jeans above the ankle.

I meet his gaze as my fingers touch his lower calf. He's warmer than I expected, and his sparse body hair tickles my palms when I drown in his gray eyes. They're attentive and bright like two ponds that have frozen over for the winter.

"I'm Cesar, and I know how to deal with minor injuries."

My fingers have been broken or otherwise injured more times than I can remember. One needs to know how to keep themselves mobile in my profession, whatever the situation. Still, maybe I'm not as professional about this as I want to be, because a part of me itches to push my nose under the folded denim and inhale his essence straight from the warmed skin.

Eli leans forward. "How? You're not telling me the full story. There's a reason you're helping me. Though... I guess I'd like to know what's wrong with my ankle first. Can you tell?"

My tongue dries, and I lean forward, eager to tell him everything. How I was at the gala because I wanted to put pressure on Sullivan over a broken promise, but that Eli freed me from the bastard instead.

He *freed* me.

Of course I'd make sure he's safe, healthy, and never suffers any adverse consequences of his actions. But now isn't the time for difficult truths. He'd be scared of the real me, so I shrug, assessing the damage to the mildly swollen joint.

"I'm ex-Special Ops." The lie rolls easily off my tongue, and before Eli can ask me a question, I adjust his joint with a decisive twist of my hands. My patient stifles a cry, but he will only get better from now on. "And this? Just a sprain. We should ice it with some snow."

He takes deep, raspy breaths because of the pain I've caused, but in my mind they transform into the sounds he'd make under me—No. That is not my objective. I wasn't supposed to talk to him, let alone get involved. It's not even Friday. And he suggested he's not gay, so I need to leave my feral instincts behind.

"Thank you," Eli finally utters and opens his jacket. "Just so you know, I'm not... I don't just go around killing people. I wasn't even sure I'd pull the trigger until I did."

"Neither do I," I say without thinking, then stall when I see his eyes widen.

Fuck.

Why am I so flustered around this guy? I'm usually so confident. Maybe it's because I'm still adrift after Sullivan's death? I hated him, but he was still a compass to guide my life. Without him, every direction is fair game.

Or is Eli my new North Star?

Everything inside me shakes in protest, because I ought to want freedom and independence. But after a lifetime of service, do I even know how to live without someone as the center of my universe?

"I've knocked them all out," I add, massaging his ankle. Maybe I don't need to, but I want to.

"Oh. Oh, that's good. They weren't evil bastards like Sullivan. I can't blame them for trying to arrest me. They don't know the full picture." Eli looks into my eyes, and I notice he has some freckles on his cheeks. I love freckles. "I didn't think I'd meet someone who hated him as well."

"Why?" I ask, shifting closer to pull my knuckles over the underside of his foot, attempting to loosen his stiff muscles. "The man was a scumbag."

Eli laughs. "That tickles! But yeah, he *was* a scumbag. He bulldozed through people and no one dared stand up to him. Those who did probably ended up in body bags. I half expected to be in one last night. I counted my chances as fifty-fifty."

Yet he still came to face him.

How sad.

But also brave. Admirable.

I take a deep breath, pushing my fingers up Eli's calf, and while I started this as a way to promote healing, I can't lie to myself and claim my intentions remain innocent. With the way he's dressed, I can't see whether he also has freckles on his neck, but I hope he does.

"What did he do to you?"

Eli goes quiet for a while, vulnerability painted all over his face, and I can almost see the pain Sullivan caused him. I *need* to know everything about it.

"I never told anyone. I couldn't. Sullivan threatened me and my dad, so we kept the secret. It's strange to be free to tell you about it. But I want to. Ready for a sob story?"

He's trying to minimize whatever happened by joking, but I see him. A man pushed to his limits by fury and suffering. And I'm more than ready to shoulder the burden.

"Tell me," I whisper and sit back on my haunches.

The scent of pine somehow feels more real now. As if we're in a cabin in the woods, far away from any pursuit, and from other people. I like having him to myself.

Eli clears his throat, and I can almost smell his uncertainty, but he starts talking.

"My family used to own a Christmas tree farm. Five years ago, as I went out with my dad to survey a part of the land, we stumbled upon people trespassing. But when we got closer to confront them, we realized they were burying bodies on our land. That, of course, was Sullivan and several of his men. Once they saw us and knew what we witnessed, all hell broke loose. I thought we'd die. They beat us up but didn't kill us. I don't know if our begging was enough, or if Sullivan's later intentions for our farm were the reason, but we swore to remain silent about what we saw if they only let us go.

"But that was just the beginning. A week later, a letter arrived with an offer to buy our farm. A bad one, obviously, but it was still enough for the rest of my family to get greedy and start pressuring my dad to sell. He... he didn't take any of that well. He drank too much after my mom's death and couldn't handle the onslaught of lawyers at our door. From family, and from Sullivan. Every day was hell, and he loved that farm, because Mom loved it, and he couldn't let it go, just couldn't—"

Eli gasps and covers his face. "Sorry. Give me a moment," he mutters through deep breaths.

There's something endearing in him being so emotionally fragile despite the murder he's committed. I've not had access to such emotion since I was a child. As soon as I was handed over to Sullivan, to be forged into his obedient weapon, any frailties were torn out of me, since they were weaknesses.

It's beautiful. So earnest. I want to lick those tears off his face and taste that pain.

To think that Sullivan and his men had driven Eli to such wrath... And then it hits me that I recall this Christmas tree farm. I've not seen Eli before. I have a great memory for faces, so I would have remembered those freckles. But I did bury a body or two on the land that used to belong to his father. Sullivan told me to treat it as his own property, that the owners knew what their land was used for, that they wouldn't object as long as I stayed out of their sight.

I didn't question him then.

I never dared question him after being punished for it once.

A deep shudder goes down my back as I remember the state of panic I stayed in for a length of time I'm still not sure of. It was dark, and by the time Sullivan released me, his men had to rehydrate me with IVs. An adult can only survive without water for three days tops, so my best guess is that I was locked up for a bit less than that.

I never disobeyed after my release, and this man freed me. There can be no greater kindness than that.

"I'm sorry."

Eli takes another shuddery breath, but has to wipe away tears when he reveals his face again. I clench my fists on my thighs, fighting the urge to pull him into my arms. Maybe that's what I get for being treated no better than an attack dog.

"Thank you. We spent over two years in a court battle with my mom's side of the family, and they were supported by Sullivan. I don't want to bore you with details. It was ugly, exhausting, took all our savings. It was just me and my dad against the world." Eli gives the artificial Christmas tree in the corner a longing glance. "At my wits end, I started telling my dad how I want to just go and shoot him. Fucking split him open with a chainsaw or smash his brains into the sidewalk. I couldn't stand that Sullivan had so much power, and no matter what we did, our lawyers couldn't win the battle."

Eli shakes his head and slouches. "Everything went to shit from there. My dad he… He had a gentle soul. When we lost everything, he… took his own life. But it's really Sullivan who has blood on his hands. He ruined everything I had. I'm not even gonna get into how my last two years looked like. The revenge plot in my head was the only thing fueling me."

"So you did plan this," I say softly and offer him a protein bar when I notice the distinct rumble in his stomach. We didn't get to enjoy our sandwiches for very long after all.

It makes me giddy that Eli doesn't hesitate to take it. Like I brought my new master a ball and he chose to play with it.

"Well… yeah. I wasn't sure I'd be able to get close enough. He's always got bodyguards around. I also considered that I might threaten him, make him beg for my forgiveness, like he made me and my dad beg for our lives five years ago. When I saw an opening, I took the shot." Eli doesn't look into my eyes as he bites into the protein bar. "I wasn't thinking. But he deserved it, didn't he?"

Confirmation shoots from my mouth so fast I'm almost embarrassed about its breathiness. I can't make myself meet his gaze, because had I been escorting Sullivan last night, the bastard would likely still breathe. I could never resist his commands, even though he wasn't worthy of me. But Eli? Eli is. I can sense it with every cell in my body.

"I worked for him once." It's not exactly a lie, since my service is now as over as Sullivan's life, but I still dread to see disgust in the gray eyes.

Eli chews slower and eyes me with suspicion that makes me want to prove myself to him. "In... what capacity?"

He won't know unless I tell him, but the obedient dog deep inside me curls up in shame as I lie. "Bodyguard. But then I—" My hand rises to touch the artificial eye. It's designed to be as realistic as possible, and since I suddenly lack the words to explain what happened, it's easiest to just pluck it out and show him.

"What are you doi—" His eyes grow wide and at first, he puts his hand on my forearm to stop me, but then he must finally realize it's artificial and lets go. "Oh. How did that happen?" His voice is so full of empathy I don't know what to do with it. I don't let anyone see my weaknesses, because in my experience they always end up being exploited. But the way he's watching me now appears so genuine I long to rest my chin on his knee and let him pet me. As if it was Friday, and I was let off my chain to seek pleasure and bury myself in the fragrant warmth of another body.

I need to stop thinking of him like that.

"Injured on the job. It's nothing that interesting."

"And he fired you?"

"Moved me to other work." More like, started ignoring my existence and the promises he made. That was why I was there to see everything unfold. "But I couldn't leave. He still owed me a final payment."

Eli laughs nervously. "Good thing you weren't on the job when I made my move. I would have probably not made it out."

A smile tugs on my lips. "Probably not. I'm happy it didn't work out that way."

"Wait." Eli squints, looking straight into my eye. "Did you sabotage that Christmas tree so it fell on the cops?"

My toes curl at the sense of pride gripping every bit of my body. Sullivan never acknowledged me like this. "I might have."

Eli chuckles. "I want to show my gratitude somehow, but I had to leave my car behind so I've got literally nothing. Too bad there's no eggnog hidden in Santa's Grotto, because at least we could get smashed before the inevitable capture by cops in the morning."

"No," I say, raising my chin to meet his gaze. I place both my hands on his knees and squeeze them in reassurance, because this is something I know. Eli freed me from Sullivan, and if I can make myself useful to him in return, maybe it will give me a sense of being done with my past life. Maybe then, I'll be able to turn a new leaf even without the tattoo I'm owed?

"No?" He hesitantly glances at my hands.

I rise to my knees and nod, because I'm more certain with each heartbeat. Eli doesn't deserve to rot in prison because of a good deed most people wouldn't dare to acknowledge as such. But I know how much Sullivan's death can mean to a man, and I'll not let that happen.

"There's a cabin in the woods. We can wait out the manhunt there."

"As in... it's *your* cabin?" Eli licks his lips, and now I want to lick them too. Fuck. He is so lickable all over. I would love nothing more than to bury my face in his armpit and rest. I can restrain myself though. I've done nothing but that all my life.

"We'll be safe there," I confirm as a plan of action comes together at the back of my mind. And just like that, I'm back on my feet, pulling him up to join me.

"I probably shouldn't trust you. But it's been so long since I've had someone in my corner, I just *want* to. Sorry I'm such a coward." His eyes are so sincere and glossy with unshed tears, it takes all my self-control not to pull him in for a tight hug.

"You have good instincts," I say, and my hands move up his arms. "I'm a stranger. But between me and the police, I'm your best bet."

"That's settled then. Let's go to your cabin in the woods in the middle of the night. I'm sure that will be perfectly safe for me." He smiles at me nervously.

I understand why he'd worry, but it's okay. I know my own intentions, and they're honest. I want to keep him safe, protect him, let the manhunt die down a little, and then we'll think about further travel out of the country.

I will *not* get possessive of him as soon as we spend a day at the cabin. And I will *not* make a move on him. Even when Friday rolls around.

Chapter 6

Eli

Deep down, I didn't believe the plan would work out. If the cops caught us, Cesar would end up arrested too, paying the consequences of taking my side. But I'm not good enough of a person to reject help when it's freely offered. So I let him lead.

A shed behind the grotto contained a snowmobile. Its absence was unlikely to be discovered until morning. By that time, Cesar and I were hours away, on our third stolen vehicle.

I don't know where my savior learned how to start cars using cables, but I don't question it as long as he's taking me away from the manhunt. I can imagine special ops soldiers are trained in things like that.

My anxiety levels after the killing were through the roof, but Cesar's presence, his confidence and leadership lulls me into such relaxation after the flood of adrenaline that I doze off in the sturdy SUV. I'm used to sleeping in a car anyway, but this one's got heated seats, a luxury I didn't even dream of.

A rumble wakes me up. I'm covered with a blanket, cozy like a marshmallow between two crackers, only my feet turning into icicles. Maybe it's good for my swollen ankle? But as I blink away sleep, a lightning bolt cuts through the dark gray sky swollen with clouds. Wet snow hits our windshield so fast the wipers can barely handle it.

It's Cesar's hands that make me worry though. He's squeezing the wheel so hard his knuckles are white. If he's nervous, I am too.

"Everything okay? What did I sleep through?" I ask and admire the tall trees. I hope we're close to that cabin, because the route ahead might become impassable with such intense snowfall. The vehicle shakes over a series of potholes just as that thought passes through my mind. I blink away the haze of sleep to notice we're going through a dense tunnel of trees that look straight out of a Tim Burton production, complete with bare witchy limbs. If we get stuck here, at least we'll freeze to death before anyone can stumble upon us.

"The blizzard's slowing us down, but we should be there very soon," Cesar tells me in a strained voice, leaning forward, as if he expects a massive grizzly to storm straight at us from the veil of snow ahead.

"I couldn't have gotten this far without you. Thank you." I need him to know how grateful I am. He has his reasons to help me, but I'm feeling guilty I slept while he drove through the night. "Us Sullivan haters gotta stick together, right?" I joke to lighten the mood and hold my hand out for a high five.

Cesar glances my way, and my heart sinks when I see that the unnatural tension is still twisting his face as much as it does the muscles in his hands. He doesn't high-five me, so I let my hand fall awkwardly. Is he regretful about helping me after all? But before I can think of a way to ask, he hits the brakes so rapidly I almost hit my head on the window.

When I look up, the headlights shine straight at a wooden porch far up a long driveway.

"We're here," Cesar mutters, offering me a tense smile. I hope the way he's acting doesn't mean he *is* a serial killer. One that takes out murderers like me.

"Oh good. Wow, and it's not just some shack," I smile back, unfastening my seatbelt. The storm outside rumbles again, and I have to fight the wind to open the car door. I'm so eager to be inside even if it's probably as cold as a freezer.

The cabin is a wooden structure, with a sloped roof, but it's hard to see much more when wet snow slaps me in the face, and a gust of wind is intent on tipping me over, into the slushy carpet covering the ground. I didn't used to be such a weakling, but the lost weight and a year living out of a car has taken its toll on me.

I'm about to dip my foot in the dense snow when a dark silhouette looms on the edge of my vision. I can hardly breathe from the sudden fright, but then I smell a pleasant, herby scent and relax into Cesar's arms.

"Hold me around the neck. We need to watch that ankle," he shouts so I can hear him over the howling wind.

I've not been touched in so long I don't know what to do with that request and helplessly raise my arms instead of following the order. "Oh? I... Oh, it's fine. I'll manage. The snow will be like a cold compress." I laugh it off, but my heartbeat speeds up by the second.

Fuck.

I have to admit it.

I've got a little crush on him.

Who wouldn't? He's so fucking competent. Bought me dinner, saved me from arrest, and made sure I had a blanket. Let's be honest—it doesn't hurt that he's hot as fuck either. I don't have to see him naked to *know* he's ripped under that jacket. And that face? He's one of those guys who walks the fine line between being ridiculously handsome and not standing out too much, with a wide nose, shapely jaw and eyes like two pieces of coal. Even if one of them is fake.

If he was a porn star, I would watch each of his movies and spend my nights dreaming about bumping into him one day.

But he's here.

He's saved me.

And even though he's likely straight, the perspective of physical closeness is paralyzing. Because what if my body reacts and that sets him off?

Would he hand me over to the cops if he knew I've sucked him off in my dreams?

I stop breathing when Cesar grabs my hands and leads them to his shoulders, and then, he plucks me out of the car, into his arms.

I gasp when he picks me up with ease. I might be skinny, but I'm still a grown man. No one ever *picks me up*. I feel like a fucking princess as he carries me up the winding driveway bridal style. The wind howls around us, and he squeezes me harder when lightning strikes again, as if he wants to protect me from that too. I could feel like prey being taken to the serial killer's lair for dismemberment, but Cesar is warm, smells nice, and carries me with the confidence of a knight saving the damsel from a burning castle.

He must have really hated Sullivan. Thinking about it makes my heart swell with pride. I did that. I killed the fucker. Maybe it wasn't *for* Cesar, but he benefited all the same. Maybe we're both knights. It's just that now I'm injured, so he needs to save me, keep me warm in the storm—

I have to stop fantasizing. I'm a homeless fugitive with only one good shoe. Reality is what it is. I probably smell. Or is the orange and cinnamon still clinging to my clothes? I can't tell anymore.

And yet, I lean into him all the same, because I've not had a hug in years. I'm so starved for this connection it's embarrassing even if Cesar doesn't know what's going on in my head. He stiffens when thunder crashes above us again, icy shards hitting my bare cheek like tiny needles, but then his shoes thud on the wooden porch, and the small cabin protects us from the elements even though we aren't inside yet.

Cesar fumbles with the keys, but once the door bangs open, we step inside.

It's not... ideal, since the place is blackout-dark and smells of frost, but I can't complain when I had a jail cell as my alternative.

"Fuck... never been here in winter," Cesar mumbles, setting me down on the couch covered with a plastic sheet.

"Thanks," I say, a bit flustered and feeling as if my debt with him is growing. I need to do something for him or I'll implode.

I get up as fast as he sets me down, and despite limping a bit, I pull off the plastic cover and look around. The shutters on the windows make the place dark, as if it's the middle of the night, but I get their purpose if no one lives here.

"Do we have electricity here? Water? Fireplace? I don't want to bother you if you'd rather just go to sleep after the drive, but I want to be useful."

Cesar is out on the porch. The wind pushes the door in farther, but I can't take my eyes away from that tall, sharp silhouette. He's hunching, as if bracing for something to dash at him from the storm. When that doesn't happen, his feet move, and soon, he's out of my sight, gone in the blizzard. Immediately, I feel a sense of loss and distract myself by searching for a flashlight. There is one on the dusty coffee table, and it comes to life the moment I flip the switch. Its wide beam reveals bare log walls. To the right of the couch Cesar deposited me on is a compact kitchen, with a small fridge, basic utensils, and a single gas burner, but before I can work out if there's anything to cook with, something growls, and the electric clock nearby comes to life.

So maybe Cesar went out to turn on the generator. This means the place might have heating other than the fireplace. I wonder why he became so quiet, but maybe he's just tired after a long drive. I'll ask him if he wants to eat when he comes back. In the meanwhile, I pick up some trash to keep myself useful. A can on the counter, an empty packet of chips. I pick up a chair that was on the floor as I explore the living room and peel the plastic sheets off furniture.

The house is utilitarian in nature. No pictures on the walls, no particular color scheme, not even a deer head trophy for some rustic character. I'm not being critical, just assessing the place that might become my haven for a while. If anything, I'm excited to sleep under a roof instead of in my car. I'll miss the few books I had to leave behind, the bundle of photos I had to remember my family by before it all went to shit. As impractical as it is,

I had a Christmas garland I made with my mom as a kid in there and a few very personal baubles. Nothing fancy, but it stings that I'll never see any of those items again.

Maybe if we stay here all the way until Christmas, I could make some decorations. Unless of course Cesar was against it. It is his place, and he does seem to prefer decor that screams I'm-a-bachelor-I-don't-need-trinkets'.

I'm about to explore farther down a corridor, when the door opens, and Cesar steps back in with the bags of our shopping in both hands. I rush over to him so fast I almost stumble because of my stupid ankle, but I'm desperate to take some of the load off him. He lifts the shopping as if I were a kid trying to wrestle a knife out of his hands.

"Your leg! Careful, we can't go to the ER right now," he scolds me before resting all the bags on the table close to the kitchenette.

Damn, we've been on the move for so long, but he still smells so good. How am I to deal with this? I look up, but the air I've inhaled gets stuck in my throat when I notice the black eyepatch covering his injured eye. It's simple in design, sleek yet utilitarian, like the rest of his clothes, and something about it is turning me on, because that strip of leather makes him resemble a Bond villain.

"Sorry. I'm hungry again. Can I grab this? Or do we have to ration?" I pluck a pack of five croissants out of the bag. The pounding against the roof intensifies, making me glad Cesar's not out there anymore. This sounds like hail, and the poor guy's already dusted with a dense layer of snow. I raise my hand, about to brush it off his head but stop myself at the last moment.

I need to get a grip.

The pastry bag rips open in my hands, and I stuff my face. Cesar's watching me, still as a statue. Did he notice what I was about to do and is now assessing whether he doesn't want to let me sleep outside after all?

An arm slides around my waist, and he leads me back to the couch, no longer frozen. "Sit down and make us sandwiches. I need to set everything up," he tells me, back to his patient self.

I want to protest, but he's soon back and places all of the food on the coffee table. "There's a store not that far away, so no, we do not have to ration." With that, he's out of the room.

I take a deep breath and make myself useful. At least he gave me a job so I don't feel like a waste of space. As I spread ketchup on a very pale slice of cheese, I'm hit by the memory of blood splattering all over Sullivan's white shirt.

I've barely had time to process what I've done. I killed a man. Or did I slay a monster? I glance at the butter knife in my hand, also covered with red sauce. Am I just a man who was pushed to his limits, or have I always had this anger inside me? If push came to shove would I stab someone to protect myself? Would I kill someone who tried to call the police on me? Or a cop?

The turmoil inside me makes me a very slow sandwich artisan, but Cesar is gone for several minutes, so I think he doesn't mind. Unless he's rethinking his life choices and considering suffocating me in a pile of snow. I wouldn't blame him. His footsteps echo behind the door close by, and I drop the piece of bread I'm preparing into my lap. Of course it has to land with the buttered side on my pants, but it's not as if I can turn back time and make myself not-an-embarrassment.

Cesar enters carrying a pile of wood. His facial expression is stern, impossible to read, so I hope for the best and assume he has resting serious face. Which, incidentally, I find stupidly hot.

"I started a fire in the bedroom already. It's small, so by the time we lie down, it should be nice and cozy there," my host says, kneeling in front of the wood burner close to the couch.

At this point, I don't need the fireplace, because hot flames fueled by inappropriate thoughts lick my neck, my jaw, and then my cheeks. He didn't say 'bedrooms'. And I highly doubt there are two singles in there. Or maybe there are, but I'm too awkward to ask about it.

"It's been a while since I slept in a real bed. Thank you. Again. Is there a shower here? I don't feel so fresh after... everything."

"There is, but you need to wait for the water to heat a bit." He nods, leaning forward and blowing on the flames. His back is so nice—sturdy, wide—I wouldn't mind using it as my anchor.

I haven't had sex for even longer than I was homeless.

How pathetic is that?

I take off my jacket, which feels like removing armor. It's old, utilitarian, in a vomit color between green and brown. I don't love it, but it's warm, and has a lot of pockets, even if it's torn on one elbow. Underneath I have a big gray hoodie which, unlike Cesar's nice fitted sweater, does nothing for my body. Not that it matters. I wish it did.

I'm so greedy. It's not enough that this man is risking his life to save me from prison, I also have to make him the object of my fantasies.

"I'm sorry I dragged you into all this. It must be such upheaval in your life," I say quietly as the room fills with the warm glow of fire.

He glances my way, halfway through closing the wood burner, and the flames reflect in his dark eye like an echo of my lust. "I'm the one who should be thanking *you*," he says, rising to his feet and approaching me.

I force myself to look up, because my instinct is to zero in on his crotch. It's been far too long since I was touched, and after he freaking *carried* me, I'm a little smitten.

"For the sandwich?" I joke and hold it out to him. The better one, without ketchup dripping out of it.

He accepts it and sits on the old couch, so close his knee brushes mine, sending thousands of fiery ants up my thigh. "No. For doing what I couldn't and taking care of that sonofabitch." With that, he pokes his sandwich against mine, as if we're toasting.

I'm so proud of myself I straighten a little as I bite in. I've not had this much substantial food within twenty-four hours for a while now. I'm reminded of how Cesar dealt with *four* cops and a civilian with a gun, and my heart beats a little faster. To have someone like that on my side? Wow. Just wow.

Unless he actually is a serial killer and I'm a sitting duck. No one will miss me but the cops itching to get a promotion following my capture.

We're about similar height, but when he sits so close to me, I'm even more aware of how much bigger he is. The jacket could have created that silhouette through good tailoring, but nope, he's just that well-built. No wonder, if all those protein bars and cans of tuna are his go-to snacks.

"You wanna go shower first? You deserve it after the drive," I say between one bite and another.

Cesar glances my way, his gaze intense as if he's trying to peek under my skin, but before I can feel self-conscious, he finishes one of his sandwiches and rises. "I just might. Won't use much water, and this way I'll make sure you don't freeze," he says and pulls off everything he's wearing on top.

I'm salivating, and it's not because of the food.

I took him for a straight-laced kind of guy, at least as straight-laced as someone who is ex-special forces can be, but his whole upper body is covered by a massive tattoo. Reminiscent of the ink I've seen on Viking culture enthusiasts, a huge tree spreads all over his back, sides, and torso. Even his arms are adorned with the ink. Woven into its leafy branches are symbols that at first glance don't seem to fit in with the main image. I spot the Eiffel Tower, as well as some other landmarks from all around the world, as if he were collecting memories. One space is notably left blank, right over the heart, but the skin below it is marked by a massive red scar descending from Cesar's solar plexus to his navel. I shouldn't stare, but at least the scar gives me a reasonable excuse. Not that I'm not interested how he got it, but I'm too busy admiring every dip between chiseled muscles, his pecs, his biceps, and oh-my-fucking-god, the V-shaped muscles at the hips? Yep, they're most definitely there too.

The fire burns behind him, his body is a work of art, the eye-patch makes him seem hot-dangerous (which he is), and I've never felt more inadequate.

He's GQ, and I'm the free local newspaper you get in the mailbox and immediately throw away.

He's the main hero of a Marvel movie, and I'm the fifth guy in the *Fantastic Four* who didn't make the cut.

He's a wolf on the prowl, and I'm daddy long legs.

Even the fact that I dare fantasize about someone so out of my league is embarrassing.

"Um… That's a big scar," I point out, and he touches it, as if I could ever make someone like him self-conscious.

"I've had it for a long time," he mutters and clears his throat. "I won't be long."

He's gone before I can apologize for daring to soil his cabin with my presence, but it's not like I can take my comment back. Couldn't I have been normal and said something like 'wow, that's some gains, bro. Which protein shake do you recommend?'

As promised, he's soon back, dressed in sweats and a long-sleeve. Is it because it's still a bit chilly, or because he doesn't want to show the scar to the weirdo who pointed it out? I'll never know. I've already finished my food, and the fatigue of our escape is catching up with me, so I'm grateful that he's willing to switch on the water for me in the tiny wet room.

"I don't... you know. I don't have anything to change into," I say before he leaves me to it.

Cesar pats a pile of clothes on top of a wicker laundry basket. I hope the towel folded alongside them is his.

The shower itself feels heavenly, but the hot water is limited so I don't overindulge, focusing on just a quick wash to be fresh. There's a mirror in the cabinet over the sink, so I do try to arrange my damp hair into something that doesn't resemble a gray bird's nest, but it is what it is. There's spare disposable razors on the counter, so I take advantage of that, since it's been a few days. I'm sure Cesar won't mind.

The white T-shirt hangs off me, and I don't know if that's hot, because it reminds me of how beefy he is, or embarrassing. The plain pajama pants have a drawstring, so I can tie them tightly enough that they don't slide down my hips.

I take a deep breath of the warm air. I can't believe I feel so good when I'm a fugitive who murdered a town *mayor*. I glance into the mirror, and I don't even feel so bad about myself for once. Yes. I did that. I pulled the trigger. I didn't cower, I didn't let him get away with his crimes, I took justice into my own hands.

I walk out with my chin high, smelling fresh, and ready for bed, only to focus on the warm light coming from under the door leading to the bedroom. A sigh escapes my lips when I imagine myself back-to-back with my hot savior, but it feels like too much of a risk, so I clear my throat and speak. "I'll take the couch." I'm about to ask about additional blankets when Cesar cuts me off.

"Don't be ridiculous. It's way more comfortable here!"

My heart is in my throat, because... what if he *does* want to sleep with me? Wouldn't be the first gym bunny who's into skinny guys he can handle with one arm.

My mind drifts off to a scenario where (oh no!) I have to pay him for protection in blowjobs. What a life that would be... I don't sleep around, because lately my life situation wasn't exactly conducive to that, but I also need a connection to feel comfortable.

And boy, do I feel a connection with Cesar even though I met him yesterday.

If he wanted to, I would.

I lick my lips and open the bedroom door with my heart beating all too fast.

Can you get a heart attack from too much excitement?

CHAPTER 7

CESAR

THE CABIN'S GROUNDED, so even in the unlikely case lightning did strike, I should be safe enough, but I can't help the throbbing sensation over my heart each time thunder rolls over the sky.

Reasonably, I know the implant in my heart must be a lie constructed to keep me in line from a young age, but my lizard brain tells me to never test that theory. With Sullivan dead, in the case the implant *does* exist, there's no one else who would be able to activate it. A storm is another matter though, as I was told lightning could affect the mechanism.

The mechanism that doesn't exist.

And yet, my body remains stiff, and I wish to burrow deep underground. Lying on the floor, as far from the roof as possible will have to suffice.

I nod at Eli when the door opens, pulling the blanket all the way to my chin. I know I've been short with him since we arrived, but I can't let him know how badly something as mundane as the weather affects me. He's here under my protection, and I need him to feel safe.

As soon as I see him, that strange bond with him flares up inside me. I'm instantly back to where I caught a glimpse of his eyes after he killed Sullivan. He was wearing that silly Santa costume, but I'd recognize those gray eyes anywhere. They pushed my split second decision. I could have either pursued him for the murder and broken his neck, or decided that he was the one who freed me from the leash of a cruel man.

I made my decision, and here we are.

I finally get to see more of him, even if in baggy clothing. He's bony but tall, his cheeks are flushed, lips a little darker for some reason. Because he's skinny, his cheekbones seem more pronounced. With the curiosity in his eyes and the way he's fiddling with the hem of his T-shirt, he reminds me of a weasel. So cute and slinky. He'd be so easy to handle in bed. I want him to gain weight for his own good, but it doesn't need to be much if he's not keen. He's perfect already. If only I could get my hands on him...

"Um... so..." And now I know why his lips seem darker, because he bites on them again. "That's unreasonable. The bed is big." Eli points to the king-size bed I'm lying next to.

By any person's standards, he's correct. No need for me to take the floor, as if I'm a dog guarding its master, but when I glance up at him and imagine how fresh his damp hair must smell after the shower, it feels like too much of a risk. I've missed last Friday's fun due to a bad cold, so my self-control might not be as tight as it usually is, and I don't want to creep him out.

Spending the night on the couch would have been a solution, but at thirty-three I know myself enough to realize I wouldn't be able to doze off in another room when Eli could be in danger.

So here we are.

The intense thunder above us isn't helping me be reasonable.

"Don't worry. You need the rest more than I do."

He walks in, taking unsure steps toward the bed. He's barefoot. I should have given him socks too. He has no idea how precious he is to me. For as long as I remember, I've been under another man's heel, and as Sullivan's killer, Eli is the obvious choice for me. I need to adjust to being around someone who isn't here to command me but needs protection and guidance himself.

"I don't have lice, you know," he jokes, but wraps his arms around himself and sits on the bed. I can't read him right now.

I lick my lips, sitting up with the blanket around me. He's close now, and I can't help but react to the scent of his damp body. "You deserve a comfortable bed."

"We'll be fine. Look how big this bed is. The comforter too." Eli crawls toward the headboard to pull on the bedding he was sitting on. He might be skinny, but I get a view of his rounded ass in the pajama pants. He glances back at me, and some hair flops over his eyes. "Or is it me? I could take the blanket, you the comforter, so we don't pull on it? Or swap tomorrow?" he's starting to babble again, and I can't help but find it endearing. Most of the men I worked with were curt. Especially with me. But he's so genuine, unsure, fragile from malnutrition and struggle.

I rise to my knees and grab his hand, leaning close. It's only now that the aroma of his skin and hair hits me with full force. He's earthy yet fresh, like a dewy clearing deep in the woods. Like moss, and wild berries, and sun on my skin.

But I don't want to lie and enjoy the comfort of his fragrance. I wish to roll over and bury myself in him, rocking my body until lightning descends on us, and we both stir, as close to heaven as a living person can get.

I let the blanket fall and spread my knees so he can see why I'd rather keep a degree of separation. I'm ready for him to recoil, but it is what it is, and he needs to know, whatever the outcome.

His eyes widen, face flushes, but he doesn't pull his hand out of mine. I'm not yet sure what to make of it, but he speaks. "Oh. I... Do you need a minute?" His eyes travel from between my legs and up to my face. "Or is this *for me*?"

I should lie.

I should deny it and leave to take care of my problem, but what is the point of that? If I'm to be around him all the time, this is bound to happen again, and we need a system based on honesty.

So I nod, clearing my throat. "I didn't want to make this awkward."

With Eli for once rendered silent, I get up, because while he needs to know, it's not like he's expected to do something about it.

The next lightning strike hits so close to the cabin, my ears ring. My heart goes frantic, and I act on instinct. I fall forward and cover Eli with my body in panic. If the roof falls down on us, at least I'll be on top. I hate storms. I fucking hate them.

"Um... it's okay," he whispers after a moment and strokes my side.

Is he... trying to comfort me? I realize with embarrassment that he must sense how tense I am, how fast my heart is beating. How useless. I'm supposed to be his protector. Someone who will keep him out of harm's way until he's somewhere safe.

And yet, it's so nice. I don't remember ever being comforted. Sure, I've fucked my way through lots of guys, and that's meant occasional cuddles before or after sex, but this feels different. Like he cares. Like he's not put off by my weakness.

When I dare glance into his eyes, he swallows, then shifts his head a little closer and gives my lips a tender kiss.

I never expected this.

Not in a million years.

His lips taste of mint yet are so soft and warm I itch to probe them with my tongue, explore and consume all of that sweet affection. I rock between his open thighs. My mind's a jungle—deep, dark, and dangerous—I can only hope he doesn't regret taking a step inside.

When he makes a little whimper against my lips, my dick twitches as if it's already conditioned to get hard at the cute sounds Eli makes. All my blood drains from my head, so I don't have the capacity to overthink how this changes our situation. I can only *feel.*

His fingers climb up my arms, to my shoulders. The tip of his tongue teases its way between my lips for a deeper kiss. His dick's rock-hard against mine. The scent of his hair, his skin. The shape of his hips in my hands when I slide them down.

He wants this. Wants me. Maybe he doesn't know the depths of who I am and what I did, but he already knows more about me than any other lover I've had.

"I'm going to eat you alive," I mumble, pulling up his top, because I can't stand another minute of it being in my way. The fabric stretches over Eli's face, but once he's free of it, those gray eyes settle on me, dark with passion. He's delectable—a young lamb separated from its flock—but I won't hurt it, not really, just tease it with gentle nips to have a taste of flesh without losing him altogether.

I want to savor this, savor *him*, for as long as I can.

I tried to keep myself in check, but that's out the door now. He's mine to protect, mine to hold, mine to fuck.

His gasps are quicker. Does he realize he's stepped into the wolf's den? Is he afraid, or does he like it here?

Eli's pupils are wide, and even his pale chest is flushed. As soon as the T-shirt's on the floor, he grabs my face and pulls me in for another kiss while he grinds his hips against me in the same frantic rhythm I am.

A hundred lightning bolts could be hitting around this cabin and I wouldn't know, because my heart is beating too loudly to hear anything other than the sounds in this bedroom.

This man. Eli. My savior. My charge. He is my whole world right now, and nothing else matters.

I grab his bottoms and drag them down, eager to touch his long legs, then cover them with love bites before finishing my masterpiece with rivulets of cum. He will be mine, and I want him to understand that.

"The way you smell… it's so damn addictive," I mumble, pushing my nose under his jaw.

"M-my smell?" Eli chuckles, and raises his thighs to rub them against my sides. One of his hands slides over my nape, giving me goosebumps when it dips under the collar of my long-sleeve and explores my back.

I nod, arching into the touch, my mind surfing the wave of pleasure as I suck on his neck and rock against Eli's erection.

He wants me. He wants to be around me. He needs me.

"I crave more." With that, I grab his thighs and pull him away from the middle of the bed, until his ass is on the very edge of the mattress. "And you?" I ask and nip the skin around his nipple.

"Yes," he rasps, watching me in amazement. "Take your top off. I want to see more of you. Please?" he adds as if he considers his own words too demanding. He has no idea. He could ask the most outrageous things of me and I'd try to make them happen. If he wants to see me naked, he can feast his eyes all he wants.

In the warm glow of the fire in the wood burner, I slide off the bed and peel my top off for his viewing pleasure. The flames color his eyes a dusky orange, making them resemble two pieces of amber when I shed my pants too, standing naked between his spread legs.

His gaze feels like touch. As if it rubs my bare skin up and down, then tickles my balls as I place my hands on his raised knees. "I'll make you feel so good you're never going to even look at another man," I say, and while I've only met him yesterday, every word rings true.

As much as I hated Sullivan, without him I was adrift, and Eli is the anchor I need.

Eli bites his lip and nods, watching me absentmindedly. His gaze moves over my forearms, my biceps, my pecs, my stomach, and lower, to my stiff dick.

"Honestly? I believe that. You're gonna fucking ruin me and I'll ask for seconds."

I feel like a predator when I smile, but he doesn't seem scared and watches me spit on my hand, then rub the saliva onto my stiff cock. It already feels better than if I were taking a moment of solitary pleasure, but while the idea of spilling myself over his skin is compelling, I want more than that. I want to feast on him, and for both of us to be addicted to each other.

His body appears even longer as he stretches out, a feast fit for a king. Pink nipples like strawberries on his cream-pale skin, and the soft skin on his stomach, presented to me in submission as if he wants me to bite into it and gorge on his insides. I take a glance at his flushed face, lips parted in invitation for either my kisses or my cock. My decision. So I look all the way back down his long torso to his stiff cock, evidence of just how excited he is for whatever I want to give.

My knees fall to the blanket, and I push my face into the soft skin of his thigh, following his scent between his legs.

I love the way he trembles under my touch, and it only makes me squeeze his flesh harder. He makes a needy thrust with his hips, but while I see his dick, and it looks delicious, my goal is lower, in the tight crevice between his buttocks. Eli moans when I make my playful bite to his thigh that little bit harder.

All my life I've had to restrain myself and act violent when let off the leash. Sex has been the only space where I can do things on my own terms. Where I'm the apex predator, allowed to do as he pleases.

"You... you look amazing," Eli chokes out, rising to his elbows to make eye contact, and I'm immediately hooked on it. Good. I want him to watch as I push my nose against the skin of his balls, inhaling their aroma, only to descend with my tongue out and already tasting flesh.

"Oh? Oh...!" Eli moans and falls back flat to the bed when I push my tongue against the tight opening into his body.

I want to know every inch of him, but this pink, soft part of him is especially exciting. It's puckered, responsive, and I can't wait to feel it squeezing my cock. But not yet. I need to whet my appetite a bit more, so I fold my new lover in half and *taste* him.

His body stiffens, then relaxes when I continue my exploration, rolling my tongue against the pliant flesh while my hands close on his ass. He's trembling. Gasping. Arching. By the time I gently nudge his hole with one finger and spit into the opening, my Eli is ready to give me anything I might ask for.

I've always loved the texture of the delicate skin between a man's cheeks, its earthy aroma, but it feels different this time, as if it's not just about satisfying my own desires but also making him feel good. Helping him relax and understand that I've got him.

I squeeze Eli's sides when I stab his relaxed hole with my tongue, but it's when I press my fingers to his taint that he goes wild, moaning as if I was already fucking him.

"Fuck...! Fuck... No one's ever..." He gasps, sliding his feet over the edge of the bed.

One look up gives me the perfect view on his long, squirming body. His dick is in the foreground, red and leaking pre-cum over his stomach, and he stretches his arms over his head, lying there and panting for me.

My tongue circles his opening as I explore the hairy skin of his buttocks with my palms. "Really? But you taste so good."

I love that I can make him so breathless and scattered. It gives me a whole new sense of power. It goes beyond the body. He's something special to me.

"Um, yeah, I... kinda washed... more. Just in case. You never know what might happen." He curls his toes with a moan when I push my tongue in again. "None of my boyfriends... yeah."

"Lousy, lazy fuckers. It should be a crime to neglect a hole this pretty. I'll be better than that, you'll see," I whisper, sucking Eli's taint as I give his cock the gentlest tug. He's so aroused I can smell the testosterone on his skin, but so am I, and while I could eat his ass for another hour, my balls are starting to ache.

Eli pushes up to see me, and his flushed face, his parted lips are so fucking hot I don't know if I want to fuck his mouth or his ass. But I'm greedy to hold him closer and I can do that better when I'm between his legs.

"You will?" he whispers in disbelief as his cock twitches right in front of my face, tempting me for a lick.

I meet his gaze, but his eyes shut when I suck his dick in halfway, sucking it so intensely, the slender body twitches under me, begging for more.

I can't wait a moment longer.

"I'll fuck the memory of any other man you were with out of your system," I rasp, crawling onto the bed, on top of him. As I predicted, it's child's play to move him around, especially now that he's so overcome with pleasure. Still, he's working with me, and moments later, he's holding himself open for me, thighs pressed to the chest. I approach him with intent, a wolf ready to consume the lamb that chose not to run from him, and spit on his hole while I spread my slick pre-cum over the head of my shaft.

I know there must be something in the house we could use as lube, but I can no longer think straight, and when Eli's glossy eyes meet mine, I know he can take me this way too.

More than that—he wants it.

I press my cockhead to his hole, and I don't know whether to look at the perfect picture it makes, or to his red face and tongue darting out to lick his lip. I've been with submissive guys in bed, but this is something else.

He seems to have completely surrendered to me. In my cabin. Hunted by cops. He has nothing. Only me. And while I'd never abuse his weakness, it's a thrill to know that I've done well enough to deserve this.

I push in with a grunt of pleasure. He's so damn tight it's as if his body is hugging my dick.

Eli makes a few whines that sound so animalistic, I'm even more turned on. He lets go of his ass to grab my arms, and we both still as my shaft sinks inside him.

"Mine," I mumble, staring at him from behind my lashes. "I won't let anyone else touch you, smell you, taste you. You belong with me."

Eli's pupils expand as if I rubbed coke into his gums, and he nods, making those little whines with every inch of me he takes.

"Yes. Oh, fuck. Yes," he utters, brows drawn, when I'm balls-deep in his inviting hole. He's gripping my arms so hard his nails dig in, but I don't mind. I want him under my skin.

"You like that?" I whisper, pressing my hips even harder against him, to push every bit of my shaft inside him. His eyes roll back just before I draw my hips back, gently rocking back and forth. He feels velvety, tight, and so damn warm I have no doubts I won't be able to last tonight. But that's okay. There will be another time to enjoy this at a slower pace.

"Come closer," Eli begs, pulling on my arm. This neediness of his is endearing. It feels like seeing the real him. I've peeled back the layers of the Eli he shows to others to get to the core that only I will own. He's panting, and the scent of his sweat is an aphrodisiac. "Fuck... you're big... but I like it."

"Secret size queen?" I rasp, lowering myself over him. And as my elbows sink into the mattress, I taste his perspiration, overwhelmed by its musky aroma. I move in gentle, long strokes, and since his body is still in the process of yielding, each thrust makes him feel more familiar.

"Ah, fuck you. I just like to feel it." Eli chuckles and I sense the tremble of his body on my dick. This is how close we need to be. One body. I'm gonna fill him with so much of my DNA we're gonna fucking merge.

The friction is almost too much to handle, and I withdraw from him. The warm air of the heated room is fragrant with the aroma of wood and arousal, but when he whines in protest, I'm quick to add more spit on my cock. When I enter him again, there's no hesitation in my actions, and he makes the sweetest of gasps, trembling as if he were already on the verge of climax.

He wraps his long legs around my hips, trying to pull me closer, and while it's tempting to play with him like a cat might with a mouse, I also want to come. Now. Inside him. Listening to his soft cries.

Shifting my position offers me way more leverage, and I lean over him, withdrawing, only to push back in, searching for the right angle. "Tell me when I hit the spot," I whisper and lick him from jaw to cheek as he wraps his arms around my neck.

He looks so out of it when our eyes meet up close. Fucking gorgeous. A unique beauty from pretty eyes to his bone structure. And every time I pump my dick in, I can see it on his face. Eli gasps, his nostrils flare, his dark eyebrows draw close.

I watch each minute expression, and I know I'm there before he even says it by the way his eyes widen, then roll back, and his moan turns into a helpless mewl.

So I speed up.

I was brought up to be a killing machine, but I might as well use that muscle control in bed. With him.

"Fuck! This! Here! Fuck me like this!" Eli begs, pulling me close.

His wish is my command and I become fucking relentless in the way I pump my dick into his needy hole. My mind is pulsing with the need to get him off mixed with my own greedy lust. It's like a beast inside me that has only one primitive purpose—to breed. Instinct drives me to his neck and I close my teeth on it without much force, just to hold him in place.

I need it with my entire being, and when my lover twitches, tightens his legs around me, and shudders, uttering a series of choked grunts, I know he's ready.

His warm, sweaty body milks my cock, as I let my weight rest on top and plow him mercilessly, just like I imagined.

It's too fucking good.

How could anyone get into bed with this man and not itch to worship him in every way? I would move mountains for him. Protect him with my own body, and pleasure him as many times as he wants.

He's mine. And now I'm his too.

I might have blacked out for a bit, because once the waves of pleasure have washed over me, I'm still on top of that prone, fragrant body, and Eli is stroking me.

His fingers slide over my back, and he still has his legs around me, either not wanting to let go, or not wanting to change position so my dick is in him that little longer. I indulge in the soft kisses he's leaving on the side of my head. I feel so... accepted.

"I've never gone bare before," he whispers after a while, seeming happy to be my mattress, because he's not pushing me off. "It's so fucking hot to have your cum inside me."

"Fuck… yes," I mumble, cozy as if his arms are my personal heaven. "There's more for you where that came from." I'm already dozing off, so fucking comfortable and satisfied I'd rather not move an inch until morning, but some things need to be said. "I'm gay, by the way."

Eli laughs out loud, and even that feels like a caress. He thinks I'm funny.

"Good to know. I am, in fact, also gay. Which makes this unexpected road trip infinitely better. Stay like this?" he asks, and I'm all too happy to melt into him.

It is only as I'm falling asleep that I realize the storm's over, and I never even noticed when it passed.

CHAPTER 8

ELI

IF THIS WERE A dream, I wouldn't want it to end.

But it isn't. I'm awake, and the hottest man I've ever met is asleep on top of me. He's heavy, simultaneously hard and soft to the touch, and the heat between my buttocks is a reminder of what we did last night.

Cesar wanted me.

He wanted me so much he initially wanted to sleep on the floor to avoid scaring me, but then I found out, and the jolts of mutual desire brought us together. It's been so damn long since I've been fucked—over a year, since my breakup with Spencer—but when he climbed on top and helped himself to my body as if it was his God-given right, I didn't have a single doubt that it was what I wanted too.

He smells like a summer breeze in the woods, all fresh herbs, with a bit of salt and musk from last night's sweat. And while I am going to need the restroom soon, I don't have the heart to wake him up after he drove me to safety, and then made sure to pump me full of cum.

I blush just thinking about it. And the way he *rimmed* me? Like there was nothing he liked better. No one's ever done that to me before, and now I know I was missing out. Such a skilled tongue. I'd chastise myself for losing my mind and going bare, but what is that in the face of me becoming a murderer and wanted fugitive?

And the things he said to me? I'd be fanning myself if my arm wasn't trapped under his delicious weight. I can only hope he meant at least half of them. No one's ever been that intense with me, not even the guy I planned to propose to one day. As if I'm not just someone who 'will do', but the only one he wants. I don't even mind if Sullivan's death is the main reason motivating his desire.

I'm wondering how much longer my bladder can last before it bursts when Cesar rolls off me and to his back, presenting me with yet another reason to stay in bed. I could admire his body for days. Too bad I'm no artist, because he'd be my new muse. I want to learn his tattoos by heart and find out what every scar is from, including the massive one in the middle of his chest.

It's time though. I ease my hand from under him ever so gently, to not wake him up and run off to the bathroom for a leak.

I take a shower while I'm there too, and as I clean myself, the tenderness in my hole reminds me of how hungry this model-handsome man was for my ass. Each lick and tease sparked fireworks deep inside, and if he only agrees to rim me again, I'll massage his feet and fan him whenever he's tired.

No one's ever been this passionate with me. I thought maybe that kind of stuff didn't happen in real life, but Cesar, my savior, made me feel like I'm the hero of a romance book being ravished by some handsome prince whose darkness can be combated through love.

I'm ridiculous.

We've only just met.

He's helping me out of gratitude and surely just likes gangly guys with long legs.

But that doesn't mean I can't enjoy it and give back.

And *oh* do I want to give back. My foot, while tender, is looking less swollen today, so I'm happy to throw myself into a whirl of cleaning the cabin and preparing the most luscious breakfast I can out of the groceries we've got.

After yesterday's storm, I was expecting to be met by gray clouds and dirty piles of slush, but instead, the sky is blue, and perfect mounds of fresh fluffy snow adorn the driveway.

It's still over two weeks until Christmas day, but I'm already starting to wonder what I could get Cesar. Since I've got nothing, no access to internet, and barely a few bucks to my name, it's probably my best bet to make something. We might be on the move by then, so starting on any handmade gift now is not such a bad idea, is it?

My mom taught me how to make origami angels and Christmas trees. Those could be arranged into a long ornament if I made enough of them. I could also make a papier mâché bauble, like one of those my family used to make for every Christmas. I'm not sure if it's a practical gift while being on the road, but maybe we'll get a van to sleep in, go off-grid, and then we could put such a garland inside.

I imagine Christmas day somewhere in the forests of Canada or Alaska, just the two of us. I could make him French toast in a skillet over a campfire outside as he prepares hot chocolate, and then we'd exchange thoughtful gifts, all to do with what we experienced on the road by that point. Maybe we could even include my family's old tradition of a Christmas morning snowball fight?

But I'm getting way ahead of myself. I'm not sure what time it is, since we fell asleep early in the morning. Could be midday. Could be three in the afternoon, for all I know.

It doesn't seem Cesar is anywhere near waking up, so I start with cleanup. With the furnishings so sparse, there isn't that much to do, and within an hour, the whole cabin (with the exception of the bedroom) has been swiped, dusted, and polished. I used an old magazine to make a simple paper chain, which I draped above the couch, then folded the paper into tree-shaped ornaments.

The sun is heading for the horizon by the time I hear movement in the bedroom.

I'm stunned when I see him in the corridor, because yes, he's that hot. I thought maybe I just over-exaggerated it in my head, but he most definitely looks like a super soldier. He's got his sweatpants on, but they sit low on his hips, giving me the most perfect view.

"Good morning! Or afternoon." I beam at him.

I'm wearing black sweatpants that are a bit on the short side, but at least they don't pool at my waist, and a blue T-shirt which hugs me. Both these items are probably women's, but are unisex enough to not make me feel weird. I didn't find any spare underwear, so I've gone commando, but I do have socks.

I added wood to the fire, so it's nice and toasty inside. Almost like we're at a couples' retreat, not trying to evade the law after my murder rampage.

Cesar watches me from the doorway leading out of the main room. "I don't know either," he admits with a smile, and my toes curl when his gaze slides down my body. Is he making sure I look good enough in different light?

Maybe I shouldn't have so much self-doubt, but how can I not, when I'm average, on the side of thin, and he—drop dead gorgeous?

"I'll make food. How do you like your coffee?" I ask, rising from behind the table. A jolt of pain trails up my ankle, but I manage to hide it from him, because the last thing I want is for him to get nothing in return for all he's done for me.

"Black," he says and steps inside after a moment's hesitation.

Butterflies rush up my throat and my neck tingles in anticipation. It's all still so fresh and new I hope I manage not to fuck it up. "Coming right up!" I all but chirp and walk over to the kitchenette. I try not to be too obvious about the soreness in my hole, which I choose to treat as a badge of honor, but Cesar can't be fooled. I'm leaning down to open the small fridge when he stands behind me and places his hands on my hips.

"Are you okay?"

"Sure. Why?" Other than being a murderer with the catchy name of Festive Fugitive. My nape tingles at his touch as I proceed to put instant coffee in his mug. He bought it, so I'm guessing that's what he likes.

Cesar hums and presses his hips to my butt. "You walk like you're sore. Did I overdo it?"

I must be going red because heat climbs up my face. I can't see him, and his presence is almost too much to handle for my touch-starved body. As soon as I turn on the electric kettle, I put my hands over his.

"Just a little. It's fine. It's just that it's been a while, but I was too horny to care."

He exhales, and his scratchy chin rolls against my sensitive neck. Fuck, he smells so good! "Might need to kiss it better later."

I get goosebumps as if he's promised to get me flowers. Which I wouldn't actually even want, but I guess he doesn't know me that well yet. Nor do I know *him* that much. I don't wanna think about that, so I chuckle and nod, because what he's saying is that he wants to have sex again. I'll do it with him any time, any day. To be wanted this much... I never thought it possible for someone like me, and the sense of pride it grows in me is addictive.

"Y-yeah, that would be... nice." I rub my thumbs over his hands, amazed I'm getting to touch this stunning human being. Me. The homeless guy with no friends.

He shoves his nose and lips to the side of my neck, making me rise to my toes with sudden pleasure, but then he's gone, as if he only wanted a sample of my scent. "Quick shower, and I'll be back. Sorry I overslept."

I spin around, salivating at the sight of that broad back covered with intricate ink. "I'll change the sheet—"

"No," he says, spinning his head my way, and the sharpness of his voice screws me to the floor. Have I done something wrong? Was I meant to stay quiet and let him have this time to himself? Spencer hated when I bothered him after work, when he liked to have solo time before bed, and all of a sudden I feel the thin ice I'm standing on is starting to crack. But before I can utter an apology, Cesar shakes his head. "Stop running around. Sit with your ankle elevated. I'll deal with the bed."

And with that, he's gone.

Now I want to treat him even more.

While I do see how changing the sheets could be a bit tricky, doing a few things in the kitchen isn't that hard. I already prepared a lot of the food before, so it's a question of arranging it on the table so it's all spread out for him when he's back.

I time the coffee with when I hear the water turn off, so that it's hot for him. I'm no house mouse, but—fuck it. Hard to be a house mouse with no house, so maybe I do like the domesticity with the right person. Just because I lost my shit with Sullivan doesn't mean I can't be sweet.

There aren't that many dishes available, but I make use of all that I found, placing hard-boiled eggs, canned peas with mayonnaise, and other simple foods in separate bowls, including a can of tuna in case Cesar wants it. By the time Cesar returns, with a towel around his hips, the spread I've prepared for him looks as impressive as it can, given the circumstances. I'm particularly proud of the even way I cut the tomatoes and how I folded the napkins.

It was a lot of work, but the surprise in Cesar's eye is all the reward I need.

His hair is now out of place, and while he's towel-dried it, small droplets keep falling to his chest and shoulders as he settles at the table, adjusting the eye-patch. "Is it some kind of holiday I don't know about?"

I start loading food onto my own plate, maybe a little too quickly but I'm starving. I wanted to wait until he got up, so we could eat together. I did grab a few crackers, but that was that.

"No, I just wanted to treat you. You already did so much for me. The way you handled those cops yesterday? Wow."

Cesar wraps his fingers around the mug of coffee and smells it, watching me so quietly my thoughts start going in circles. Is it too much? Does he think I'm being a suck-up?

The tension inside me loosens when he smiles and takes his first sip. "It's been a while since someone praised me like this."

Be still my heart. It's like giving a treat to a dog that's been kicked all its life.

I have a massive bite of my peanut butter and jelly sandwich, while with my other hand, I'm already shoveling a big spoon of peas in mayonnaise onto my plate. "I also..." I don't know if it's appropriate at the table. Another ex of mine, Terry, liked to fuck as much as any other guy, but didn't like discussing sex and would get upset if I attempted to bring it up. "I never came with no hands before."

Cesar freezes with a peeled egg halfway to his mouth, and meets my gaze. He blinks, puts it down, and wipes his hands on the towel around his hips. Fuck, he's so handsome. I don't deserve him.

"So... I assume you mean you enjoyed that?" he asks, as if he hadn't eaten my ass like it was his favorite dessert. Guys like him are never shy, but he seems almost... uncertain.

He was definitely confident last night.

I smile at him, giddy that he didn't shut me down. "Well, yeah. That was so hot. Was there something you liked most?" I ask, bump his foot with mine, then fill my mouth with the peas. It only now occurs to me he might find that combination strange, but what's done is done.

Cesar licks his lips, resting his elbows on the table. "Do you want to have sex now?"

I sink back into my chair, unsure how to answer that despite arousal already blooming in my balls, as if his desire is my on-switch. "Do *you*? I mean... maybe. But I'm also really hungry? Is that okay?"

Cesar frowns. "Why would it not be okay? I just thought.... that's why you mentioned what you enjoyed." We both stare at each other until he stuffs the egg into his mouth. "I-uh... I liked how you looked at me," he says. "And that we can do it whenever we feel like it."

I beam at him, mindful of keeping my full mouth closed. He liked the way I *looked* at him? Throw snow at me, because I might be melting. "I just wanted to be accommodating. In case you really wanted sex and it was a dealbreaker," I say as soon as I swallow.

He watches me intently with his eyebrows drawn, as if he wants to read my thoughts out of my skull. "It's not. I want you to *want* me. What do you mean when you say 'accommodating'?"

I get flustered when I realize how that might have sounded. "Not that I'd do it even if I don't want to. I just..." I look up from his navel, all the way to his face. "I can't imagine ever *not* wanting you. So if you wanted sex, I'd be up for it. I have quite a high sex drive, and I lived like a monk for far too long. I kind of... I'm not always good at initiating things, so I just wanna say, if you feel like it, go for it." I barely hold back a smile when I notice him spreading his thighs a little. His eye is now darker than black. It's a void leading straight to Hell's Circle of Lust.

His nostrils widen as he leans in, taking in air, as if he wants to smell me. "So what you're saying is... if I feel aroused, I should use your body to get off?"

I have to fan myself as I grin at him. He gets it. My heart beats faster, but we need to eat first. Unless of course he does decide to act on my declaration. I love that it's up to him.

I really fucking do.

"Yes," my voice comes out raspier than I expect. "I want to satisfy *you*. It turns me on. If the impossible happens and for some reason I can't or don't want to, I'll just say so. Otherwise..." I wink at him and lick jelly off my top lip. "You know."

He's watching me like a lion getting access to live prey for the first time in years. Eggs disappear in his mouth so fast it's almost as if he wants to get the breakfast done and bend me over.

Hot.

"I like this whole talking thing," Cesar tells me, moving his hand across the table to settle it on top of mine.

"I ask about stuff to get to know you better. And sex is part of that, you know? I'm aware that the way we met is super weird, and the situation is highly abnormal, but we're alive, not in jail, snowed in in this lovely cabin, and Sullivan's dead. What's not to like?"

Cesar chuckles, then laughs so hard some of the coffee spills down his hand. But instead of getting frustrated over burning his fingers, he knocks the mug against mine, as if we were toasting. "To the man who made it happen. I'll rim your tight hole whenever you want me to, so you always remember I appreciate what you've done."

I'm sure I'm blushing, but I grin back. It's so hot that he likes it. "I had to do a lot of things myself from a young age, you know? So maybe that's why I figured in the end that if the court won't convict him, I just have to roll up my sleeves and get to work. Honestly? I didn't actually think I'd do it till the last second. Still can't believe it."

"That's why you prepared all this food for just one meal? To celebrate that it happened?" Cesar asks and gestures at the full table, eating with more vigor.

A deep sense of satisfaction fills my chest. "Maybe? Unconsciously? My mom always did that. Not just celebrate with food, but she'd make it special. Even if it was just pizza and cookies, she'd take it all out of boxes, put it on nice plates, maybe light some candles, put on music." I clear my throat, hoping it's not all too sad for him, but I want him to know me. "When she died I tried to continue with that for me and my dad. He wasn't doing so well even before… you know. Her death really hit him hard, and he battled depression, so even as a kid, I tried to do what I could to brighten his day."

Cesar watches me in silence, then places his hand on my forearm. "Thank you for wanting to brighten mine. I don't often have company."

"How so? I imagine a guy like you would always have someone vying for his attention." A compliment, but I also do want to know so much more about who this amazing person sitting across from me is. If he's ex-special forces then what does he do now? Was bodyguarding for Sullivan his last job? He did say he was let go after he lost his eye.

Cesar shrugs and leans over his plate to shovel tomatoes into his mouth. The glow of the lamp above adds warmth to his skin tone, until it's almost honey-like, and I kind of wish to taste it.

"Maybe. I try not to overthink it."

Okay, so I'm getting that he can be a bit closed off. Makes sense for someone who was a soldier. "If that's what works for you. I, on the other hand, overthink *everything*." I laugh, but it's actually kind of a problem. "Like whether you like my new clothes, or if you'd be mad I grabbed them myself. If you like the food I prepared. Where we will go and how I will live there as a wanted man. Can police dogs sniff out my scent over snow? Should I keep my gun or throw it away? Was it okay to use the old bleach over the tiles in the bathroom, or should I have used something more environmentally friendly? Do I talk too much?"

"I like your voice," Cesar says, sipping his coffee almost as if he were trying to hide behind the mug. "I also like your new clothes, so I'm not mad, even though I prefer you naked. The food is delicious, but we need chicken for protein. You don't need to worry about the future, because I will take care of you and make sure you're never caught. The Festive Fugitive will forever remain a mystery. I'm not sure if police dogs can 'smell over snow', but don't worry about it. They lost our scent when we started using cars. Keep your gun. Bleach is fine. You don't talk too much. You are nice, and I like your company."

My heart beats faster, and this time not just because I'm horny. I can't believe he's not only listened to my babbling, but also remembered every single thing. "That's so reassuring. My mind can be such a mess. How about your family though? Sorry for asking straight up, but if we're going off-grid..."

"There isn't anything to talk about, really," Cesar says curtly, and I find myself sinking down the well of anxiety again, because who says stuff like that to someone's face unless they want to dismiss them or point out that a line was crossed?

I shouldn't feel this hurt when he's just reassured me. Not everyone has to share as much, but yeah, I am a little hurt, because last night he told me that I'm his. How no other man will exist for me, yet now I'm getting shut out.

Then again, maybe his whole family died in a car crash, which then prompted him to join the military? I could see him being not ready to talk about that, and it's no fault of mine.

I gobble down another sandwich to relax before I speak again. Last thing I want is for him to decide I'm too needy. "I'm sorry I'm coming on so strong. It's been a while since I got to talk this much. I've been living out of my car and feeling kinda invisible. And it's been even longer since I had a boyfriend, so sorry if I'm a bit feral."

The silence following that last sentence is like a growing hollow inside my chest. Anxious, I look up and meet the single black eye in Cesar's handsome face.

"Is that what we are?" he asks, each syllable smashing the hopes I've built up in my stupid head.

My stomach sinks and I can't meet his gaze anymore. "I don't know. Maybe? We could be. We'll see. No need to put a label on it," I fake a cheery tone when on the inside I want to scream into the void.

What the fuck was I thinking? Of course he declared things last night in the heat of the moment. Maybe he even meant them at the time. Why do I have to keep pushing like this? Just like with Sullivan. I couldn't let go, and now the life I knew is over. Not that there's much to cry about there, but I can't go to *prison*. I wouldn't last two weeks.

I can see how Cesar might like me, find me convenient in a non-cynical way, but why did I have to say *boyfriend*? Why would someone like him choose to tie himself to a ball and chain like me?

Cesar grins and reaches for the peanut butter before proceeding to gather a big spoonful, which he then shoves into his mouth. "Okay," he mumbles.

I bite the inside of my cheek but keep my expression neutral. "I'm full. I'll start cleaning the dishes if you don't mind."

Cesar shakes his head. "No way. You need to rest. I'll do it."

In truth, I only wanted to do it to escape the uncomfortable situation and not cry in front of him over something he's allowed not to want. I know I'm an emotional wreck and he's not responsible for my feelings. My own insane life choices have led me here.

I get up, grabbing a rice cracker. "Thank you. I'll go check out the snow before the sun sets. There's piles of it," I fake a cheery voice, but it might crack soon, and I need to be out.

Cesar frowns and points toward the corner. "Be careful. It's best if you don't get off the porch with that injury. But there's warm boots you can take by the door. We should trash your old pair."

I nod, touched that he remembers the problem with my old shoes. I rush away to get dressed, put on the warm winter boots that fit my foot as if I'm Cinderella, and I step into the cold air, which doesn't ease my frantic mind.

I know I'll fall for him all too fast and then suffer inevitable heartbreak.

Fuck my life.

CHAPTER 9

CESAR

PLEASURE SHOULDN'T COME FIRST, yet Eli's words refuse to leave my head as I finish my meal. In my mind, I already have him on his knees, tonguing my cockhead, but he's worked so hard to prepare this amazing meal. Cleaning up is the least I can do.

I ignore my hardening dick and rise, gathering all the dishes. Eli will soon be back, and when I take him up on the proposition that's burning me from the inside as if I've swallowed a pint of embers, I want this place to be spotless for him.

It's not even Friday, but Sullivan is gone, and my new sun wants me to lavish him with attention, so I will. That's what he needs me for, apart from protection, and I want nothing more than to fulfill his wishes.

It's strange how long he's been out in the cold. The only thing still keeping me from going to check on him is the last cup I'm washing. He's not from anywhere in the south, so I'm not sure why he seemed so excited about snow.

From the moment I took him under my wing, I've barely let him out of my sight. Even when he showered, I listened to the sounds of water, reassured that I know where he is. I don't know why. I can't explain it. It's a much more intense need for protection than it ever was with Sullivan. Like I'm growing anxious when he's not around.

As soon as I put down the cup, I rush over to get my boots and a pair of sweatpants, because I can't take this separation any longer.

The fresh scent of the forest hits me with so much intensity it's distracting, and the darkening sky makes it harder to work out where Eli is, but I finally spot him. He didn't stay on the porch, as I suggested.

He's much farther away, and there's an obvious trail in the snow where he's waded through it. Close to the treeline, he's... is he making a snowman?

"Eli?" I call out, admiring the heaps of untouched snow surrounding the cabin. It's bitterly cold, but I won't freeze if I stay outside for a couple of minutes. Him on the other hand? The man's barely got any padding on those bones. No wonder he's eating mayo and peas just to fill that void.

He turns almost too fast. The dusky light catches wet streaks on his cheeks. He rubs his eyes the moment he spots me.

"Oh, hi. I... I'm not finished," he points to the large snowman with twigs for arms as if to distract me, but I still catch the stifled sob.

What. The. Fuck?

I'm moving before I can even consider going back for a jacket. The cold pinches my bare arms, but I don't care.

Eli is unwell, and I'll be damned if I let that stand for a moment longer than necessary.

"Is it your leg?" I ask, following his tracks in the snow.

"N-no. It's just… allergies," he says and rubs his face again with fingers so pale they look blue in this light. Was he making this snowman with his bare hands? What is this madness?

"You will make yourself sick!" I won't let this continue. If Eli needs to sulk for some reason, he can do that on the couch, resting his ankle and covered by a thick blanket. I don't bother asking for permission before picking him up, but his slender, elongated body melts into mine despite the tension pulling at his muscles.

If he said I'm free to use his body, I'll carry him whenever I damn well please.

He gasps, but doesn't protest, just sobs again, making all the hair on my body bristle in panic. I *need* to know what's going on and fix it.

He's unhappy, and he chose to hide that from me, because he's a good person and doesn't want to upset me. I've fucked up. I don't yet know how, but I have, and I won't find peace until I know.

The cabin feels shockingly warm after the brief time outside, so I kick off my snow boots and carry Eli to the couch. He's so cold to the touch it's fucking with my head, and once his boots are off, I sit alongside him and pull his head to my chest before covering him with one of the folded blankets. "You'll be comfortable here. Give me the wet jacket."

He takes it off with another sob. "I'm sorry. I'm so dysregulated everything overwhelms me. I promise I can be normal."

A sharp pain passes through my chest, and I kiss the top of his head, then breathe in his lovely scent. "I'm sorry. He deserved to die, but it must still have been a shock. But don't worry. I'm here to listen."

I forgot he's not like me. He can't kill someone and forget about it by dinner time. There's a gentleness about him that I need to protect.

Eli stares up at me and I'm so desperate for him to stop crying that I want to kiss his eyeballs. "Ah. Sullivan? No. He did, he really did..." he mutters, and I'm at my wits end.

If it's not that, then what is it? I've never had a boyfriend. I don't know how to provide emotional support. I wasn't even allowed to make friends. This is uncharted territory for me, and this inability to decide what I've done wrong is killing me.

"I'm sorry... Just tell me what went wrong, and I'll never do that again," I promise and pull his face close. My tongue tastes his tears, and while I hate that he's upset, their flavor makes my toes curl.

His gaze meets mine from up close, his expression cutting me so deep I could probably extract the implant out of my heart if it actually exists. "No, it's stupid, I... I'm the one who is sorry. I know I'm too clingy. My exes said that, some of my family said that, and here I am again, feeling sorry for myself because you don't want to be my boyfriend after one fuck. It's fine, really."

I stall and pull away, with the salty flavor still lingering in my mouth as the world around us fades. "But I thought you said... we *were*...boyfriends," I mutter, now even more confused. "I don't understand. Do you want us to be or not?"

He stares at me as if I've just showed him that the puppy he thought was mauled by wolves is alive and well. "But then you asked if that's what we are, and you sounded sceptical. Like I got ahead of myself but you didn't want to be rude."

Anger claws its way up from deep in my chest, because he didn't get here on his own. The people who called him clingy and refused to give him what he needed made it so, and this sweet, sweet man deserves better.

He deserves *me*.

I shake my head. "It's my fault. This is very new to me. I wasn't allowed to date in the past, and I might blunder again, but I promise that I'll try my best to make you happy," I say softly, and my heart constricts at the sight of the subtle change in Eli's vulpine face. "And you're not 'clingy'. You're lovely, and excited, and that's hot."

I can almost smell some of the cortisol leaving his body. He sniffs and rubs his face, but there's no new tears, which reassures me. "Why were you not allowed to date? Were your surroundings that homophobic?"

I feel ridiculous. Of course a normal person wouldn't understand. I've already lied to him about my profession, and it's not as if anyone polices how much sex soldiers have in their free time. There is no good way to answer this question, and I shrug, feeling the weight of my embarrassment drag down my shoulders.

"It was… a matter of discipline. When I worked for Sullivan, he wanted me on standby at all times. I would only have sex on Fridays and was meant to use the rest of the week for self-development and training," I admit, looking away from him. Living it doesn't mean I don't understand how insane that all sounds. There's a reason why I've never revealed this to any of my hookups, but as embarrassing as it is that I let someone dictate such intimate details of my life, if we are to be together, then I want Eli to know.

He reaches for me from under the thick blanket and strokes my side with his cold fingers. As though I'm the one who needs comforting when he was the one crying his eyes out. "Oh my God... Cesar. That's messed up. I didn't know it was possible, but now I hate Sullivan even more. Why didn't you quit? Did he have something on you?"

More than Eli can imagine.

Everything.

My whole life.

Loyalty.

The muscles in my face twitch, and I shrug. "I know this isn't normal. But now he's gone, and you are here—" I swallow, moving my gaze up his chest. "I was raised in his household. I didn't really have any parents," I add, hoping it would clear things up for Eli without forcing me to say in what capacity I worked for Sullivan, or how he obtained my services.

"I'm so sorry, Cesar."

His touch, while cold, soothes the storm in my heart, and I find myself drowning in the softness of his big gray eyes. Something's off. He and I might have only just met, but recognizing patterns has always been a part of my job, and he can't hide the shift in his mood this time. "What is it?"

Eli swallows and won't look up any more. "Is this why you... had sex with me? As like... a reward for what I did?" I spot a tear sliding down his cheek again, and I need to put out this new fire fast. Seems my Eli has some self-esteem issues that go deeper than I could have imagined.

"No!" I blurt out, cupping his face. It's hot to the touch yet soft and sweet like a warm marshmallow. "You're amazing. So tall, and slender, and you have that sexy low voice," I tell him, swallowing when I run out of breath. "You're so funny, always talking before you think, and your smell makes my cock so hard I wish I could rub myself all over you. I want to have you. And protect you. And I want to fuck you every day, not just on Fridays."

I'm relieved that I must have said the right thing when a little smile appears on his lips. "You don't mind that I'm gray? Doesn't feel like fucking an old man in a young man's body, like some kind of messed-up Benjamin Button situation?"

How can I not laugh?

It bursts out of my mouth, and soon I'm shaking with the need to shed tears. "Don't be ridiculous. Your hair is like silver and gunmetal. It's beautiful," I say and pull him into a deep kiss.

How is this happening?

What are the odds that in a world so full of Sullivans and those who want to be them, I happen to end up with someone who's anything but that. All sweetness. Not even a drop of bitterness.

I love seeing his smile widen and promise myself to be more attentive so he never loses that spark. Even his fingers are getting warmer.

"Or like a very hot pigeon?"

"I don't fuck pigeons," I say, and when the air around us sparks, my hands dive between his thighs and open them in a motion so delicious, I find myself salivating. "But I want you, and you did say I can have you anytime. If you let me, I will protect you, and make sure you're happy," I whisper, trying to rein in the intense emotion buzzing in my chest.

Our gazes are locked as Eli leans back, letting me spread his legs as wide as I wish to.

"And you'll be my boyfriend?" he whispers, not even blinking as he watches me.

I'm already so much more than that. There's no word for it.

My own breath scalds my insides as I look back. "I'll be *yours*. And you will be mine. Only mine. Every day. Whenever I want."

He likes that. I can see it in the way his eyes glaze over, how he nods, and how he spreads his thighs in silent invitation.

CHAPTER 10

ELI

I CAN HARDLY BELIEVE this emotional rollercoaster I'm on.
First, I had a lovely morning, then I wound myself up in
a twist by misinterpreting Cesar's words, and now we're
back to touching and kissing, my attraction to him even
stronger than before.

He's so... set on me. It both calms me down and turns
me on. I don't have to overthink the sex either, because
he means what he says, so unlike my past boyfriends who
played games with my heart.

Why else would he be risking everything for me?

Spencer didn't bother to do my part of the house
chores when I broke my leg, and here is my dark prince,
carrying me around as if I'm made of spun sugar, saving
me from a lifetime behind bars—

Every muscle in my body relaxes when Cesar pulls my
ass to the edge of the seat and presses the lower half of

his face to my crotch, breathing me in through the fabric. His eyes roll back, as if getting high on my scent, then he pulls on my bottoms, revealing that I'm not wearing anything underneath.

"Good thing I got you some underwear," Cesar breathes, tossing my pants and boots aside.

"You did?" I blush at the idea that he's bought me something that personal. With Cesar between my legs, I'm getting hard fast. I can't resist him, and I don't even try. What's the worst that can happen? He'll lock me up in this cabin forever? At least I'd be safe and well fed. And well-fucked.

He nods, his dark hair tousled and still damp to the touch. When did I reach to his head? I have no fucking clue, but he moans, and licks his way up my cock as if it's his favorite meal, so he must not mind my touch. His chin has grown enough stubble to scratch my cockhead when he leans forward, popping his head under my top.

My toes curl. My nipples pebble.

And when something tickles my tender hole, my body jerks up, already engulfed in fire. I might be tender down there, but if he wants to, I'd let him have another go with me. It's like a drug that a man like Cesar wants me.

I make a needy moan when he sucks in half my dick. So hot, warm, wet. And while he's teasing my ass with his finger, his other hand also delves under my hoodie to greedily squeeze my pec. I can sense how much he desires me in his every touch. The synapses in my brain are short-circuiting in response to his scent. I meant it when I told him I'd be up for it whenever.

The scent of burning wood, and the aroma of orange and cinnamon clinging to the jacket I took off, combine in the warm air of the cabin, making my head spin.

This man will either take me to safety and a life of love and pleasure, or will be my downfall. Either way, I'm taking that leap.

His finger is wet with saliva when it finally pushes in, and I find myself arching, my back and thigh muscles rigid by the time I bottom out in Cesar's mouth. He feels incredible—all heat and sturdy flesh, and while I'm the one being pleasured, he never lets me entertain illusions about who's in control here.

Cesar is the one who decides how deeply he sucks me, when to tease my prostate, and when to leave me wanting. I can barely take it, but in spite of all my begging, he keeps pushing me to new heights of arousal, until I'm so horny that an orgasm crashes over me unexpectedly.

It's like tumbling down a mountain, and by the time I find myself wrapped in his arms, limp from exhaustion, I feel like I've just climbed Mount Everest, and he's welcoming me back home.

I'm tender all over and make little moans as he strokes my sweaty back under the hoodie. I can hardly think after my orgasm, my mind an empty road with tumbleweed rolling across it.

"That was so good," I whisper to make sure he knows how much I appreciate him. He might have said I'm not clingy, but he has no idea how much I already want to attach myself to him. I want to sleep with him spooning me, I want to eat breakfast sitting in his lap, and watch movies with his dick in my mouth.

I want to become a part of him, for us to be entwined so inseparably that he can't imagine a life away from me anymore.

His lips taste of my cum, and I give a breathless laugh after licking their plump flesh.

"Happy to be of service," Cesar teases, but I'm back to peak awareness when he places my hand on his hard dick.

Of course he's still hard, and I've neglected him!

I meet his gaze. He might only have one eye, but it's so attentive and always focused on me. I squeeze his cock with a groan of pleasure. "How do you want me? You've not had my mouth yet," I offer, but it isn't selfless. I'm dying to taste him.

Oh, he likes that. I can see it in the way his eye darkens further, black as a drop of tar when he chews on his lip and moves to straddle me.

"What exactly did you say? However and whenever I want?" he whispers before pinning me to the couch with a fast yet intense kiss.

I miss his hot tongue as soon as he backs away. Overwhelmed by how he now towers over me, I swallow, glancing at him as if he's my new God. Whether he's the one love-bombing me or me falling all too quickly, I don't know, and I don't care. My heart is raw, and he can eat it like that if he wants to.

"Yes," I say, moving my hands up his sides. He's so fucking sturdy. "Fuck my throat raw if you feel like it."

He growls, squeezing my flanks with both hands, as if he's trying to restrain himself. But there's no need for it. I want him. I want *this*. And I want him to want *me* most of all.

He licks me across the lips, then grabs my jaw hard and slides his tongue in, probing, testing my wet mouth, and incredibly, a jolt of arousal trails down my balls. But then he's up, one hand on the back rest right next to my head, and I only get to see his purple shaft for a moment before it splits me open.

I look up, doing everything I can to let as much of his cock in fast, but everything happens so fast I choke a little. I hope my eyes communicate that I don't want him to stop.

He's big.

I'm no newbie to giving head though, so I take a deep breath through my nose and relax for him. My fingers gravitate to his hips, because I adore touching his body.

My eyes tear up, but I still see him throw his head back in pleasure, his Adam's apple pronounced as it bobs. He's so damn handsome. I can't believe my luck.

"Then I'll make you mine. I'll make you the perfect fuck sleeve for my cock. And you will love it so much you will beg if I forget to feed you a daily helping of cum."

That voice. It's pure sex, and intoxicates me like a well-distilled spirit when strong fingers cradle my head, holding it at the angle he likes.

I zone out as if his words alone push me into a reality in which I've been his for years, taking load after load, whenever he wants to finish inside me. Maybe I'm being stupid, having those kinds of fantasies about a man who could overpower me so easily, but I want the danger. And I want a guy so pumped full of testosterone, he wants to fuck me twice a day.

His cock thrusts into my throat time and time again, and I wouldn't dare defy the strong hands holding my head in place. I'm exactly where I should be—mouth open and ready to swallow his load. I'm so desperate to find out how it tastes. I hope my mouth is nice and hot for him, that he likes the way I stroke him with my tongue. That he enjoys seeing me like this, because my face is already damp with tears and saliva, and if he keeps riding my throat so roughly, this is how he will see me every single time.

"That's good. You're such a hot mess, Eli. But you love it. You love servicing my cock, don't you?"

I hum, sending vibrations down his shaft, but he keeps talking, fingers wound into my hair.

"That's right. Keep me satisfied, and I'll keep you safe. I'll make you my little prince, the happiest man alive, but in bed, your holes are mine."

Oh fuck. Oh fuck. I might be getting hard again.

I make a little moan and nod as much as he allows me. It doesn't feel like just dirty talk. He means it. He's not toying with me to throw me away. Maybe he's as crazy as me?

I suck him harder, hugging his cock with my cheeks, and in turn, he makes the hottest fucking moan and plows my mouth even faster, his balls slapping my chin time and time again. It's such an obscene sound, but I love it, because it means he can't help himself around me. I'm stroking up and down his thighs when he grabs my hands and forces them behind my head. In this position, using my trapped wrists as leverage, he saws into me a few final times.

And then he's coming down my throat so hard I have cum rolling from my lips and down my chin. Maybe I have coughed a little, but only to remind him that he needs to finish *inside*, as he promised.

Salty, a little bitter, but because it's *his* cum, I already love it. If I could see his cock, I'd stare at that beautiful monster without blinking, but since it's in my mouth, I look up at his face instead.

Cesar is so handsome. He could be a serial killer, and I'd probably just say everyone has flaws. He has an irresistible aura of confidence, a great cock, and the way he wants me is like an aphrodisiac injected straight into my veins.

"Swallow it all, greedy boy," he grunts, closing his eye in bliss.

That's it. Enjoy yourself in my body, I think, watching him stand over me with his eye closed. I can't call needing to keep my mouth this wide open comfortable, but I would have gladly let him have another go if there was still some cum left in him.

He seems to be done though, and pulls out of my mouth before descending to the couch right at my side.

I'm so disheveled, my jaw aches, but I instantly put my naked legs over him and wrap my arms around his neck. We stay like that for a while, his hand lazily sliding under my hoodie to caress me to his heart's content. He has no idea how starved I am for affection.

When I find my voice, it's a little raspy. "How does it feel to fuck on a Sunday?" I tease even though what he told me about his connection with Sullivan is fucked up. I wish I could shoot the fucker again.

His eye opens wide, sharp as an arrow headed straight for my heart. "It... it's amazing. I feel as if you sucked all the tension out of my body," he adds, offering me a roguish smile that makes him look like a main character from one of the pirate-themed romance books my mom used to have in the attic.

"And on Fridays... how did things look for you?" I ask, desperate to know everything about him.

Some people dislike sharing, but he smiles and pulls me into his lap, as if he is as greedy for my touch as I am for his.

"Bars, saunas, apps. I liked going to orgies, because they made me feel like I got the most out of that one night," he says as if that was everyone's idea of weekend fun.

I'm no prude, but heat still crawls up my neck when I imagine him at an orgy, fucking three guys in a row. He *could* have the stamina for that. "Oh. And... is that something you're very into? Orgies?" A cold knot tangles in my guts. I don't want to share him.

He shrugs, burying his face in my cheek and breathing in my drying sweat. "Not particularly, no. But I only had Fridays, and most people don't have enough stamina to match me."

I smile at *my man* and stroke his hair. "I think I might. You're gonna have to test it. So no boyfriends?" Which makes me both sad for him, and kind of giddy I'm the first.

He shakes his head before sampling my lips with the tongue he opened me up with in preparation for the face-fuck. "No. What about you? Did you leave anyone for me?"

"No, I've been on my own for over a year. Living out of my car hasn't exactly been conducive to a relationship. Or I was just depressed about it. So sorry if I'm too needy—"

"I like it."

I swallow, smiling at that reassurance. "I've had a lot of sex, but other than once, always with a boyfriend. I get easily attached," I confess even though it's like giving him ammo he can use against me. Somehow, I feel I can trust him not to. But maybe I'm stupid and naive. I've been burned three times, and yet, here I am, ready to give away my heart again.

He nods, gaze so sincere I wish to hide in its shadows. "I feel attached to you too."

"Maybe it was meant to be then," I whisper and leave a tender kiss on his lips. Just last night I was panicking about how much hotter he is than me, and yet now, I'm not self-conscious at all. He makes me feel comfortable as if I've known him for years.

Cesar sighs. "In that case, I'll test your stamina every day."

I stroke his face and raise my eyebrows. "What if you hit your limit first?"

He leans into my touch and licks my fingers, as if he can't help himself. "Is that a challenge?"

"Maybe. I just... We're snowed in now anyway, but you will need to go back to work at some point. We probably can't be here forever?"

Cesar frowns and tucks my head under his chin, as if he can't bear the idea of letting me go. "Forever? No, but once the trail is no longer hot, we should move on. I have a place in Alaska."

I hug him tighter. Could this possibly work? I don't want to get my hopes up, but my heart already beats faster. "Oh? And you'd take me there? Is it safe? What would we live off? I'm sorry I bring nothing to this equation."

"You're bringing yourself. That's not 'nothing'," Cesar says in a firm voice and gives me a soft kiss. "With Sullivan gone, you're the only one I have to answer to, so I'll take you there, and we'll start fresh. I'll take care of you."

My breath catches. I was always the one to give my past relationships my all. I don't even know how to accept so much, so I lean in to kiss him again. I hope that communicates my feelings. No one's taken care of me for so long.

He's perfect. Just *perfect*.

CHAPTER 11

CESAR

As long I can remember, my life's been guided by strict schedules and demands I was expected to fulfill. I didn't have vacations, holiday breaks, nor weekends off. There were only Fridays, given to me by Sullivan in my early twenties when he realized he'd not be able to keep me in check if I couldn't let off steam once in a while. Now I feel like every single day is Friday.

No, better than that, because I'm no longer guided by the urgent need to feed my soul with enough substance to last me a whole week. Eli sleeps in my bed, shares my meals, reads to me, and laughs at my jokes. He's always at my side. Attentive. Sweet. So goddamn *good* I dread the moment he finds out how I served Sullivan. I do hope it never happens, but the possibility is like a splinter stuck in my heel.

I'm not used to being around another person for so long, but I enjoy his chatter, his smiles, the way he always forgets that he should rest his leg and starts trying to do things for me. I might never be capable of loving him the way normal people do, but I want to stay at his side, make sure he's comfortable and enjoy the affection he's offering me so freely. That's so much more than I ever hoped for already.

He's so grateful and praises me for *everything*.

I washed the shower? Incredible.

I peeled his eggs? Amazing.

I prepared his cold compress? I'm the best boyfriend ever.

The clothes I bought for him? Perfect choices.

I showed him how to handle his gun? I'm so knowledgeable.

Not to mention the compliments on how hot I am, how good I smell, or some minute detail, like him loving that some beauty spots on my back form the shape of a cat.

I don't know what the future holds, but each day I spend in his company feels like a life won.

I told him there's a pretty lake nearby, and he instantly wanted to go, so I reminded him he couldn't walk that much with his ankle still healing. Maybe I'm a bit too precious with him, but how can I not be? He's the apple of my eye. So when I saw his disappointment, I knew I had to get him to the lake *somehow*.

I found old sleds in the shed adjacent to the cabin, cleaned them up, and took him for a ride through the forest. I've never seen anyone radiate such pure joy. After all he's been through, losing his mother, his father's suicide, blackmail and harassment by Sullivan and his men, shitty boyfriends and homelessness, somehow he's still so resilient and positive.

Even when I drew the line at engaging with pre-Christmas celebrations, he just took it on the chin. If I didn't have such a knee-jerk reaction to his request, I would have probably even complied, since letting him make ornaments and cutting down a tree wouldn't hurt me in any way. But Christmas was never a good time for me. I didn't elaborate, and he didn't push. And now, I'm feeling guilty over saying no.

I'm desperate not to be a disappointment to him, so it soothed my soul to see him enjoy our trip to the lake, as if he were a kid visiting Disneyland for the first time. It's quite the walk back and forth, but I am strong, and my muscles have been itching for a workout anyway.

Clouds are gathering above us in a promise of more snow to come. On one hand, being at the cabin with Eli, my *boyfriend*, is an amazing experience, but I wasn't expecting we'd be here this long, and we're running low on food. We are snowed in, but I guess if push comes to shove, I'll make the trek to the closest shop on foot. I should be able to go there and back within a day.

My stomach rumbles with hunger, prompting me to speed up the hill where the cabin is located. My nose and cheeks feel like bits of ice, and I can't wait to thaw close to the fireplace while we both fill our stomachs.

"Will you have tea or coffee?" I ask, making a mental checklist of what needs to be done for our meal to arrive at the table most efficiently.

"Hot chocolate?" He grins at me, tucked into a waterproof sleeping bag like the most handsome of worms.

He's also wearing the new clothes I got him, and a warm woolen hat. At home he sometimes wears my clothes too and it's so hot. Especially if it's a sweater that barely covers his ass. Just yesterday, he did that to tease me on purpose. I walked up to him, bent him over the back of the couch, and when I realized he had no underwear on, I fucked him right there and then. As promised, he's always up for it, and that's so hot even thinking about it makes me horny. He gave himself to me completely, and perhaps I don't deserve it, but if he's willing to offer me this much power and trust, I'll accept it and make sure he never regrets his choice. I'll make him so happy all the suffering in his past will be meaningless.

If I'm lucky, maybe he won't even find out about mine.

"With marshmallows and syrup?" I ask, parking the sled in front of the steps leading to the porch. We have excellent weather, and we both take a moment to take in the snow flickering in the golden light of the sun. But then I pick him up, still in the sleeping bag, just throwing him over my shoulder.

It's almost a shame we'll have to leave this place.

I'm halfway to the door when Eli speaks. "Am I now more of a worm or a larva?"

Stalling, I focus on the tips of my boots to think, because this surely is a trick question. "Um... definitely a larva, since you will soon turn into your sexy, slinky form," I respond, hoping he'll like that.

"But what if I don't and I stay a larva? Would you still think I'm sexy?"

Taking into account that he sucked me off at the lake while bundled up in this cocoon, should I say 'yes'? Or does he mean an actual larva?

"Are you saying you want to stay a burrito for the fore-seeable future?" I kick the door open and turn sideways, so no part of his body hits the doorframe.

He groans as if it's me who isn't making sense. "No, I mean would you love me if I was a worm? I mean... *like*, or find hot. Or if you did already love me, would you continue feeling this way when I was in worm form?"

He must be fucking with me, because how does this question make sense in a world where people don't just *become worms*, but I go with it, like I do with everything else he brings to the table. I might never be able to love him, but I care for him, cherish his presence, and desire him more than I've ever desired anyone. I want to make him happy, and him being a worm wouldn't stop me. Maybe it's nice to fantasize of a world in which I'm capable of loving him.

"Would you still have your face?" I ask and toe off my boots. "Or do you mean you'd be the size of a worm? Because I could work with that."

"No, I'd be a worm. I wouldn't speak, and I'd be small, and just writhe around in your hand." He snickers, so at least I know we're fooling around about this, and it's not some trick question deal-breaker like that time when a hookup said they wouldn't have sex with me if I wore black socks. I thought it was a joke, so I wore black socks, and he just walked out on me, ruining my Friday.

"Well, I'd fatten you up, so you're nice and thick. And then, I'd swallow you, so we can always be together," I say, placing him on the couch. When his eyes open wider, I lean in to kiss his nose, so he knows I'm not being serious either.

Eli stares at me for a bit, but nods. "That's actually kinda romantic."

I pull his hat off, but he's already unzipping himself from the sleeping bag, so I'm guessing he's not all about staying a larva forever. I did consider going with it a bit longer and feeding him. As soon as he's out, he gets up to kiss me.

"Thank you for taking me to the lake, that was fucking fantastic. I'll need to commemorate it somehow. I'm just really hungry."

"Didn't I give you enough protein yet?" I ask, swiping my thumb across the sweet lips that sucked out all my juices during our walk.

"Barely. And you know how hungry I can get." He wiggles his eyebrows to make sure I get the double meaning.

I know I'm hot to a big part of the population, but it's his desire for me that makes my heart beat faster. It's him I want to serve and please. I've been conditioned to love and obey my former master, a fact I must begrudgingly accept about myself. Are my feelings for Eli only an extension of that training? A sense of loyalty to the man who killed my tormentor? Or are those emotions genuine? Does it matter when it's not an obsession I wish to curb?

As soon as I see him go to the kitchen, I'm borderline offended, because I offered him the drink, and I'll make it for him. Along with the foods I've learned he likes most.

"You need to rest," I protest and follow him. "On the couch!"

He sighs, but doesn't put up a fight. "But I feel guilty that you're doing everything."

"We've been over this. It's my job to keep you safe and comfortable, so don't complain that I'm not like your lazy exes," I say and open the fridge, collecting everything I need to make sandwiches.

Eli glances over the back of the couch with a smile. "Okay, but you have to tell me if you feel I'm not doing enough. I guess I can hardly believe you're this perfect. I keep waiting for something terrible to happen."

There it is again, the uncertainty I need to weed out of his heart. I'm loyal as a dog, and he treats me with a kindness no one ever bothered to show me. How could I ever think badly of him?

"I like taking care of you. It keeps me busy," I tell him and start heating the water for our drinks.

"Hmm... I might get it now. Is it the special forces training? You were taught to protect, and you can see I'm particularly useless, so you feel the need to save me?"

I shake my head and lather the bread with mayonnaise. "You're ridiculous. This costs me nothing. I do it because I want to. Because I want you to be comfortable."

It's so strange how he can fully understand that when it's him doing something for me, but finds it so hard to accept care. At least he seems to think about it before he turns on the TV.

I check news about the manhunt on my phone, but I don't want him to obsess and be stressed about it, because then he comes up with stupid ideas. The last one being that we should set up traps around the cabin. We agreed he gets to check the news once a day, and he was fortunately fine with that. Even said that being here is a digital detox.

The screen awakes, and lo and behold, it's another segment on the Festive Fugitive which is what they call Eli despite knowing his name and identity. Every day, some new facts from Eli's life get pulled out into the open, and I don't like it. The less is widely known about him, the better.

"Has the culture of the interwebs invaded our real lives too much?" the anchor asks, looking straight at the camera. "For a long time now, we have discussed how the anonymity of the internet causes people to ignore social boundaries and tell others things they never would have in real life. This case shows how far this can go. Even the name, 'Festive Fugitive' is disrespectful to the victim and his family. Search engine results display pages upon pages of memes and videos presenting the murder of Arthur Sullivan as a joke—"

"The first amendment guarantees people the right to free speech, but is this a worthy use of that speech?" one of the commentators on the screen asks before shaking his head.

I'm too busy with food preparation to keep watching, but a third voice joins the same discussion I've heard more times than I care to.

"The investigation into Elijah Ward's motive did reveal that Mr. Sullivan wasn't the person the public knew him as, though. Several bodies found on the grounds of his property? An underground room with torture devices? Who knows what else the police haven't even disclosed? I'd bet my arm that Elijah was a victim of Sullivan's. If anything, he saved those who Sullivan would have hurt in the future."

"Let's not get ahead of ourselves. The Festive Fugitive is hardly some angel of vengeance—"

"How would you know? The case has too many unanswered questions."

"We still shouldn't use silly terms like Festive Fugitive when we talk about murder."

I turn to glance at Eli who doesn't even blink, glued to the screen as if it's hypnotizing him. I heard about the discovery a few hours ago, but I didn't want to rattle him before our trip to the lake. I know all about that underground torture chamber and what else Sullivan hid.

I've been there many times, though only once as a victim.

"Did you hear that?" Eli whispers absentmindedly. "People will find out who Sullivan was."

But when I try to answer, he shushes me, desperate to intake all that the news has to offer.

The show's moderator turns to the camera. "It's true, there are many questions left, so who better to illuminate us on them than someone who knew Elijah Ward best? Let's hear from Spencer Shaw, his ex-partner."

Spencer?

Spencer? That piece of shit who couldn't be bothered to take over some of Eli's chores when he was sick?

The butter knife drops from my hand, and I gravitate closer to the screen, my muscles like stiff leather. I sense the tension in the room as if I could smell the cortisol spiking in Eli the moment that fucker appears on screen.

Spencer is your average Joe-type with a pleasant smile, but his eyebrows are drawn together, as if he were a funeral director trying to express both sympathy and sorrow at the same time. He's even dressed in a black suit for this remote interview.

"Thank you for having me. It's so tragic. I've been trying to piece everything together for days now. I'd say it's such a shock, but it's not when I really think about it. Elijah has expressed his violent urges to me many times. We argued about that a lot, actually."

Eli jumps up and stands on the couch with his face going red. "You motherfucker! Violent fucking urges?"

I cut his legs from under him and use both my arms to guide his ass back to the seat, because I am not letting him injure himself over this. But I understand the frustration of being accused of things that just can't be true.

Eli is a good person—a lamb hurt so badly it snapped and spilled the blood of a wolf. He doesn't deserve to be besmirched on live TV. Especially by a selfish lowlife like Spencer, who never treated my Eli the way he deserves.

"That's so interesting," the anchor says. "He has no prior criminal record, and appeared to have led a peaceful life before becoming homeless."

Eli lets out a sound I've not heard from him before. Something between a growl and a rumble deep in his chest.

Spencer goes on, and even seeing his face is making me jealous. This fuck not only touched Eli, but also made him miserable. And now he's spilling his version of events on national TV.

"Depends how you define 'peaceful'. He couldn't hold down a job half the time. I told him after he lost the court battle against Mr. Sullivan, that he should let it go, focus on getting his life in order, but he wanted to take law into his own hands. I, of course, thought he was all talk, or I would have reported it. He did have a tendency to blow things out of proportion."

The anchor nods with a serious expression. "Do you have any idea why he might have chosen to dress up as Santa Claus to commit his crime?"

Spencer shakes his head. "He always had an unhealthy obsession with Christmas. I couldn't take that, and his violent fantasies were getting too toxic. I feared for my safety. In the end, I had to end that relationship."

Eli screams out in fury. "He fucking didn't! He fucking used me until I had no more to give. And then he hit me, so I dumped him and walked away! But *I'm* the violent one?"

My skull feels like it's about to crack. On the screen, conversation continues, but all I can see now is the raw fury and regret on Eli's vulpine features. He's raising his voice until it's so shrill I worry his throat's going to be sore.

I want to protect him from those violent emotions, from feeling slighted, and from the rat playing the good guy now that it's offering him a moment in the spotlight.

"He did what? Hit you?" I ask, gesturing at the TV.

"Just once," he says as if that makes it any better. Eli takes a deep breath, but the hurt is so obvious on his face I'm losing my mind. I need to do *something*.

When the screen fills with the grainy image of Spencer's self-important pout, raw hate flashes through me like lightning. It's about to switch off my heart, and the only way to not let that happen is to put a stop to this bastard's lies.

Breathless and drunk on my own rage, I take two steps and slam my fist into the TV, making its back hit the wall. For a second, I'm shocked that I did it, but then I punch the screen again and again and again, until I can no longer see Spencer. There's steaming green jealousy in my actions as well, but the wrath I have for that fucker outweighs it. When I imagine this bastard hitting Eli I want to travel to where he lives just so I can put my hands around his neck and strangle him to death.

Spencer's managed to upset my Eli from hundreds of miles away, even though he's a worm unworthy of stepping on.

I'm heaving when a hand on my arm pulls me out of my stupor.

"Cesar? You're bleeding, come to the kitchen," Eli whispers, and when I see him standing, guilt slashes through me immediately.

"I told you, you shouldn't walk so fast," I mumble and lean down to pluck the TV cable out of the outlet, so it stops hissing at me.

"It's fine, my ankle really is a lot better. Did I... make you angry?" he asks, looking more resigned than scared, as he leads me to the sink, but what do I know? I'm not that good at reading people's emotions.

I used to be better at controlling my own too. Was it because I was afraid of punishment? Now that Sullivan's leash is off, I can express myself more freely, but is it such a good thing?

Am I unhinged?

Could I... hurt Eli?

It's just a thought, yet it feels like a punch to the gut, and I fall to my knees, struggling to catch my breath.

I want what's best for him. He does not deserve to be around someone he fears.

How is it that I try so hard yet always fail at doing things right?

"No... no, of course not. I'm sorry. I really am, Eli," I whisper and press my lips to his warm fingers.

He scoots right next to me and strokes my head. "It's okay. Sometimes I get really angry too. I'm glad I don't have to see his face anymore. Maybe if it was my TV, I would have done the same."

I don't remember feeling like this before. My chest feels like it's about to burst. It's a bad feeling, full of anger at everyone who's ever put their hands on Eli, but also at myself, because now he won't trust me either. "I just... you were so upset, because of all his lies, and when you said he punched you, I imagined it. I couldn't stand that he's not here, so I can twist his fucking head off," I growl and push my head at Eli's chest. "He doesn't fucking deserve to live! How dare he? How dare this bastard raise his filthy hand at you?"

These emotions in me are so new, so raw, I'm afraid they will scare Eli off. Sullivan always punished displays of feelings until I no longer knew if I had them. I was built to attack and maim. Even when I protected Sullivan, it was out of duty, not because I thought he deserved it. I don't know how to handle the tenderness inside me. Am I too broken to accept Eli's affection? Do I deserve it?

Eli's soft kisses soothe my pain like a cool compress to my swollen heart. "Maybe I should have taken him out as well? He hit me after telling me my plans to kill Sullivan were stupid fantasies, that I couldn't deal with violence. When I argued I could, he punched me. Out of nowhere. As if to show me. I didn't fight him, because I knew it was over that moment. I packed the few things I had and left."

Spencer needs to die. I don't know how and when, but I will make it happen. I feel dirty after just listening to that story, and poor Eli lived it.

"No one will ever hurt you again. I promise."

I know I'm mumbling, and he probably thinks I'm not making any sense, but every word leaving my mouth is a hundred percent sincere.

"Not with you protecting me, that's for sure." He smiles and gives me one more kiss before forcing me up. "Come on, let's get those hands under water. I can't stand watching you bleed."

The best I ever got from Sullivan was a sneer and "*go clean yourself up*".

It's been such a long time since I last felt another person genuinely cared for me that I don't fight him any longer and follow.

With blood thumping in my ears it's almost as if I'm submerged in water, because every sound is muted, even Eli's sweet, gentle voice. Still, I try not to make a fuss and let him wash my bleeding hand in the sink. I've already made our afternoon into enough of a mess.

Now that Sullivan's torture room is on my mind, I can think of only that as I watch my bloodied fingers over the metal sink, watered down red rivulets disappearing down the drain. Several times, people I had to deal with would crack after a smashed finger or two. I'd then supervise the hand getting cleaned and patched up in some strange dance of bad cop/good cop all in one body.

Eli stroking my back brings me back to reality. "I'll go get the first aid kit. Stay here."

I nod, my throat tight as if I'm unable to speak. I shouldn't have reacted so violently, because of course it might scare him, but without the threat of Sullivan's wrath, I'm dysregulated, like a piano that's still playing but which badly needs tuning by someone so much gentler than Sullivan.

"You're good. You don't deserve needing to deal with any of this," I mumble as Eli returns with the red box.

He gives me a kiss, then proceeds to disinfect my knuckles with the efficiency of a nurse. "You're also good, so *you* deserve being taken care of too."

"Am I?" I ask without thinking, but when he starts wrapping my hand with gauze, I don't try to stop him or protest.

He's so damn handsome when he's focused, with silvery hair falling in his face like fancy thread.

"I don't know what you've been through as a soldier, but you are good to me. I'm a killer, no matter how much of an awful human being Sullivan was. And you think I deserve a clean slate. Why not you?"

He has no idea, and if I have any say in it, he will never find out, so I shake my head and put my arms around his slim form. We have been together like this for only a week, but I already find his scent so calming in its familiarity. It stands for peace, and laughter, and sweet moments in bed, and I can't imagine ever tiring of it.

"Were you scared of me?"

Eli sighs and holds me close. I don't recall ever being held like this. A soft hug that's not foreplay but genuine affection. "A little. You're a big guy. But it only took me a moment to see you weren't mad at me. Do you struggle with some kind of PTSD? You must have been through a lot."

Do I? I have no idea if such ideas can be applied to a life as fucked up as mine, so I shrug and seek the comfort of his warm neck. "Sorry. I'll do better."

"You're allowed to feel things. We'll work it out."

My eyes itch in a way I don't understand until I realize that for the first time in years, I might be almost-crying. It's like Eli is now pulling the sled and I'm allowed to just sit there and accept his help, tightly wrapped in a warm cocoon.

I feel ridiculous. A man like me—a ruthless killer who took more lives than I can remember—needing to be coddled. I haven't let myself be like this since my parents left me at Arthur Sullivan's home all those years ago. A part of me wants to reject Eli's care, but he's so focused I fear taking this away from him would be inappropriate.

So I let him lead me to the couch, and then stare at what's left of the TV while my Eli fetches the food I prepared.

He shuffles about while I focus on the bare wall stretching above the wrecked screen. Is it fair that this is how I'm making Eli spend his favorite holidays when even that maggot Spencer did not deny him Christmas decorations?

"Do you feel happy with me?" I ask when Eli sets a plate in my lap.

He sits next to me and stays silent for a while. My instinct is to feel hurt that he can't give me an immediate answer, but I appreciate that he takes time to think about my question.

"Yes. The situation is tough, I'm a wanted man, I committed a terrible crime, but with *you*, I'm happy. I don't know what the future holds, but I want to grab as much joy with you as I can. I love getting to know you, how thoughtful you are, how exciting it is to be with you. You actually listen to me."

There it is, this kindness I don't deserve.

Without thinking, I rest my head in his lap and twist my body, so my face is pressed against his stomach. "I'm sorry I said no to your idea of decorating. I wasn't thinking about what you need then, but we should do it, if you still want that."

"Oh? You just had such an intense reaction, I didn't want to pry, especially when you said you grew up in Sullivan's household. Couldn't have been very festive, and it is your cabin." But he's perked up. He wants this. Of course he does.

I was so selfish to say no.

Arthur Sullivan's home was decorated like wealthy people's houses in the movies. That was the first thing I noticed when my parents brought me to him. But while I was playing with a wooden train and stuffing my face with candy cane, they left without a goodbye, and the whole first month in my new master's charge was painted with the same red, and green, and gold.

"Could we not use traditional colors?" I suggest while he eats, stroking my head as if I were his pet. He even leans down to kiss me between one bite and another.

"Sure. Any you'd like? It's not like we have a choice here though. We'd be improvising anyway. I was thinking we could use all the old magazines you have to make paper chains, and we could go gather lots of pine cones? You've got string and glue as well. We could make some collages, glue them onto cardboard, make a pseudo-gingerbread house!" The excitement resonates in his voice, but with my head so close to his chest, I hear his heart beating faster too, and I love that its rhythm sounds joyful.

"Yes," I say, so very eager to please him. I will gladly spend the next few days getting calluses from folding endless amounts of paper. "And you'll need to choose which tree I should cut down."

"Christmas was always such a magical time at my home. Especially before my mother died, but I tried to make it work with my Dad too. Maybe if your memories of Christmas aren't so great, we can make new ones together?" He kisses me ever-so-gently that my toes curl and my knuckles no longer hurt. I know I'll be fucking him like a beast tonight, yet right now, it's so good to be coddled a little.

Maybe if I replace the loneliness of the year my parents left me behind, and all the solo Christmases in my past with beautiful Eli moments, I'll be as excited about next December as he is.

I nod, closing my eyes.

If I could choose to love, if my heart wasn't made numb by my upbringing, I would be already falling in love with him.

CHAPTER 12

ELI

A few days after Cesar agreed to give Christmas decorations a shot, our cabin is filled with paper chains, the smell of fresh pine from the tree he cut down, and a dog house-sized gingerbread house made of cardboard. Did we make a glory hole in one of its walls? Yes. Did Cesar fuck me with half my body inside and half sticking out through the window? That's for me and Santa to know. We'll have to see what he categorizes as naughty behavior.

Safe to say, Cesar got into decorating, but it's the fact that we're doing it together that's the real expression of Christmas spirit.

It's getting warmer, and new snow hasn't piled up around the cabin for two days now, which makes me hopeful that our food stores might soon be restocked. But not today. Today, I'm minding a stew on the cooker while Cesar chops wood into chunks that will easily fit into the burners.

I still can't believe a man like him is so into me, but despite my protests, he's trying to do almost every chore, just so I don't put my healing ankle at risk. It's so cute I want to kiss him all over.

We'll have to leave this cabin at some point and risk venturing out, but I already know I'll miss the coziness of it. After a year in my car, I appreciate the roof over my head, the warmth, the fresh bedding, not worrying where my next meal is coming from, and most of all, the lovely warm body I can cuddle up to at night.

I taste the stew to make sure it's okay, and turn off the gas. Maybe it's a bit of an excuse to go see Cesar, but I spotted that he left his bottle of electrolyte water, so I'll go take it to him. He's very serious and particular about his food, which is no surprise after one look at his body. Other than doing things around the house, he also has a morning exercise routine that lasts two hours, then an afternoon one, and I saw him using one of the large trunks in the yard for strength training. The man is a *machine*.

I get dressed and walk out with his bottle, excited to see him as if we didn't live together. We even shower together "to *save hot water*", but we both know it's to be close all the time. The shower is also a place where I'm least shy about being rimmed, and Cesar never fails to make me sing in the tight space, his face buried between my cheeks until I can't bear it any longer.

The memory of him then finishing inside me this morning brings a flush to my cheeks. I put on my coat and step outside, heading for my kinky lumberjack.

"Aren't you thirsty?" I ask, and when he glances over his shoulder, I lift the bottle, prompting him to smile.

I lean over a pile of cut wood and hand him the drink. The snow is melting, the sun is out, and he's got his jacket open, revealing the tight T-shirt underneath. Damn is he dreamy. I love trailing kisses down his powerful chest and worshiping every inch of him.

Who would have thought this could be the outcome of killing Sullivan? It's almost as if fate has rewarded me for a job well done.

He grins and takes the bottle from my hand, before spilling the red liquid into his mouth as if he were starring in a commercial and needed to make drinking look *sexy*.

"Oh, that's so good. Thank you," he says and gives me the sweetest of kisses. As if I'm not a fugitive he's hiding. "Have you eaten?"

I wink at him. "If you keep asking me this often, I might start getting suspicious that you *are* a cannibal."

He shrugs, enjoying another gulp of water, and when he turns, the sun shines through his hair in a way so picturesque I wish I had any kind of artistic talent to capture the image forever.

"I'm trying to fatten you up for your own good."

A nasty feeling curls in my chest. "Oh? You said you'd like me as a worm, but now I'm too skinny?" I try to make a joke out of it, but I'm suddenly self-conscious.

Cesar laughs and places his cool hand on my shoulder. "I would like you in any form. As a worm, without any of your limbs, you name it, but you are underweight. That's why you get tired so fast, and why you get ill as easily as you said you do. I want you to be in optimal health."

I frown at him. "No limbs? Here I was, worried you consider me too bony, but now I'm thinking you want to suck the marrow out of my arm or something." It is reassuring to hear though. That he likes me as I am. His enthusiasm for me shows every day, but I'm allowed to be a little needy sometimes.

"No limbs, no tongue, no hair. I don't think there's anything that would make me stop wanting you," he says and cups my face with icy cold fingers.

My heartbeat speeds up, but just as I'm about to speak, he clasps his hand over my mouth and makes a shushing sound while pulling me close.

I knew he was strong, but the way he holds me now offers no give whatsoever, as if he has steel instead of bones.

I trust him so much I have no instinct to try getting away. Maybe he spotted a cop car already headed up our driveway? I've noticed his hearing and his sense of smell are incredible. As my eyes search for what he's seeing, I freeze, not even breathing anymore.

A whole pack of wolves, must be at least a dozen, are passing our cabin on the other side. They move close to the trees, but I can see each one so clearly. As panic settles in my bones, Cesar whispers right into my ear. "Don't be scared. They can't smell us from here, because of the direction of the wind. They likely wouldn't attack two grown adults, and even if that happened, I would protect you. Just watch. Aren't they beautiful?"

I have never seen so many wild animals from up close, and as his words sink in, I relax, letting myself just enjoy the sense of wonder as the pack trails past us. Minutes feel like hours, but when they're finally gone, Cesar's hold on me eases, and he kisses the top of my forehead.

In all my adult life, I've never felt so safe, and I let myself enjoy the moment. My stupid doubts whether I'm too skinny forgotten, I indulge in the love I find in his arms. I know it's too soon to say the L-word, so I settle for 'like', but it's love that I feel so very deeply. Maybe we've not known each other that long, but it's been more intense than any of my relationships.

Cesar *would* stand between me and a pack of wolves. I wholeheartedly believe that.

The table inside is prepared for our evening meal, and while Cesar is still insistent on doing most of the chores, he lets me handle the food tonight and sits in his usual place with a wide smile. He's about to take the first spoonful in his mouth when he freezes, eyes darting toward the door.

"What is—" I try but he silences me with a gesture. It takes a moment longer, but I too recognize a distant buzz, and my stomach plummets. Someone's driving toward us.

Cesar grabs my plate and stuffs it inside the nearest cupboard, leaving only his within sight, then dashes toward the trap door leading into the attic. He's tall enough to grab the foldable ladder attached upstairs and drag it down.

"Get in there, and whatever happens, do not reveal yourself," he says like the man who first brought me here—curt, tense, and uncertain where he stands.

I can't believe our idyll could be cut short so fast. I give him a desperate look, but he's the proficient one, so I won't be arguing, and rush up the ladder.

I just hope it's a friendly neighbor here to tell us the road is not covered in snow anymore, not a SWAT unit.

CHAPTER 13

ELI

IS IT COPS? THE real owner of this place? I have no idea, but Cesar hasn't disappointed me yet, so I crawl away from the ladder he's pushed back in after me and reach into the toolbox resting next to the trapdoor. My fingers tighten on a wooden handle, and moments later I pull out a hammer with a flat face on one side and a claw on the other. It's the same one Cesar used to hang up our Christmas decorations. I don't think I could efficiently defend myself with it, but its weight still feels reassuring, so I take it with me.

I regret leaving my gun downstairs, but it can't be helped now.

There is a small window in the roof, overlooking the front of the cabin and the driveway, and what little light it lets in reveals the massive amount of dust floating around me. Its dense cloud contaminates each inhale, but sneezing would reveal my presence, so I pull up my T-shirt to cover my nose and shuffle forward. I pop the window open almost all the way just before the roar of not one but two cars dies.

My hand freezes in the air, as I worry the men exiting the two vehicles in a hurry might spot me, but they are all focused on Cesar, who steps from the shadows of the roof's overhang as if he were expecting guests. One of the vehicles is a bright yellow SUV, the other—a red truck. Neither looks like a police car, since even plain-clothes officers tend to drive vehicles in neutral colors.

For a moment, I hope it's a group of tourists who've gotten lost in the woods after taking a wrong turn, but if that were true, they wouldn't all step out at the same time, nor would they come so uncomfortably close to Cesar.

Paranoia weaves itself through the folds of my brain, because what if the cops have tracked us down somehow? No, that doesn't make any sense either, since none of the men are openly holding firearms. Not to mention that considering the high profile of my case, wouldn't there have been a helicopter landing here as soon as the police figured out where we are?

Maybe they aren't here about me? After all, this is Cesar's place, and with the aggressive edge to the movements of the strangers, I'm suddenly terrified they're going to take him away from me. It's selfish, I know, but I can't deny that the thought is there. If those people are cops, I could take all the blame and deny Cesar had any knowledge of my crimes, but what if—

"We couldn't reach you for almost two weeks," a man in a blue winter jacket says, standing just two steps from my man. "Have you been watching the news at all?"

There's anger in his voice, and I hug the hammer to my chest.

"My phone got fucked, and there was no way to leave this place until today, because of all the snow."

One of the men, a tall redhead, takes a sharp step forward and doesn't collide with Cesar only because the stranger who spoke first stops him by extending his arm. "So you spoke to Mr. Sullivan, broke your phone immediately after that, and then buried yourself here? You really expect us to believe that?"

Sullivan.

A name that makes my mouth dry, yet Cesar's calm as ever. "Let him go, Lyle," he says, gesturing at the redhead in a way that oozes familiarity. "I actually have very valuable information."

The body language of the men transforms, visibly relaxing, but I'm struck by the sudden realization that Cesar might not be on my side after all. He's admitted working for Sullivan, those men clearly know him, and what if he's kept me here to further his position in their ranks? It wouldn't have to stop him from fucking me while he waited for the snow to thaw.

And I let him.

I started having... feelings for him, because who wouldn't when he treated me better than anyone before him?

How could I have been this naive when I've only just met him?

Typical. I always get in too deep, too fast, and choose the wrong guys.

"Since when are you the information guy, huh?" the one called Lyle asks as the redhead gravitates toward Cesar. "We're here because you can gut ten armed guys stuck in a room with you. Sullivan might be dead, but you will continue doing as you're told."

It's such an offensive thing to say. Cesar's angry—I can see it in the way he squares his shoulders—but just as I expect him to drag Lyle by the collar, he swings his right arm, and the axe he used to cut our firewood with splits the head of the man standing farthest away from him.

Air gets stuck in my chest when Cesar's other hand swipes close to the ginger's throat, and the front of the poor bastard's white jacket changes color to a bright red.

I can't fucking believe this.

This man, who saved me from the police, and who was inside my body this morning, is a dangerous maniac. He didn't kill the policemen who accosted me back in town, just knocked them out, but the sight of blood spilling on the snow makes my stomach revolt. Cesar is so calm and collected about this.

My palms sweat around the hammer. Despite the compulsion to shrink and disappear from sight, to trust that this is only a glitch, and that Cesar's true self is the man I've spent the past weeks with, turns out I actually have *some* self-preservation instinct.

Below, Lyle spins out of Cesar's way, and with the four men below locked in a chaotic fight, I grab the lower edge of the open window and take a step onto the ledge outside. I know it runs along the whole roof, and with the snow now only a thin layer, I might be able to move to the back of the cabin and disappear.

"You fucking feral monster! No wonder Sullivan kept you on a leash!" Lyle yells, and I can't help but look back. Even if I made such a bad romantic choice, my heart screams not to leave.

I turn my head in time to spot Cesar grabbing the head of another man and slamming it against the hood of the car so hard blood spills over the polished yellow. When the guy waves toward Cesar, trying to grab him, Cesar pulls his head up and slams it into the car again, somehow with even more force. This time, the guy slides off the vehicle and into the snow.

Is this really the man I've fallen for?

But if he's doing this to protect me...

Lyle takes a step back and fiddles with something in his pocket, his face redder than the blood surrounding them. It must be a gun, but the other goon next to him is faster. As soon as he pulls out a firearm and aims, Cesar is on him, a wolf cornered yet fighting with his teeth bared.

The gun goes off, my heart stops, but Cesar manages to kick it away in time, so he's not shot. He uses his bulk to throw himself at the shooter, and as soon as Cesar has him on the ground, he grabs his head and twists it with a crack. There's no hesitation. He's done this before.

Cesar turns to Lyle, bouncing back up, but the stranger pulls out a... piece of paper? He's standing with his back to me when he reads out a nonsensical combination of words.

Cesar freezes.

Then drops to his knees in the wet mud.

"That's more fucking like it, you murderous dog! You will do as I say!" Lyle yells, breathing hard, and leans forward, placing his hands on his thighs. He was terrified. But now he isn't.

He pulls out a gun.

What did he do to Cesar? My man is panting, covering his head with his arms and rocking back and forth like he's having a panic attack or some kind of PTSD reaction.

All because of something this fucker's *said*?

The cold air fills my lungs as I inhale and squeeze the hammer. Maybe I have a death wish when it comes to the men I pick, but I'm not leaving him.

CHAPTER 14

ELI

I HAVE NO IDEA what's going on. Nothing about the scene playing out below makes any sense. Even the blood staining the snow to form a surreal pattern seems out of place outside the cabin where Cesar and I have led such a peaceful existence for what feels like weeks.

But one thing is certain, whatever's happening below is not right. Cesar killed those men to protect me, and he doesn't belong on his knees, twisting in pain. He deserves so, so much better, and while I know he would want me to run, I can't leave him like this.

In one quick move, I slide down the roof like snow sports are in my nature. All I can see is the gun pointed at Cesar, and the monster who's turned my man into a helpless creature. So what if Cesar is a beast too? He's *my* beast.

When I drop to the ground, my fall is cushioned by snow, but my barely healed ankle gives way with a nasty crack that makes bile rise in my throat. Heat shoots to my face as I stifle a cry of pain, stumbling toward a catatonic Cesar and the man watching him with strange satisfaction.

My heart thrums like an engine at full throttle, and I'm spurred on by the memories of Cesar smiling at me when he showed off his first Christmas paper craft.

The guy turns his gaze to me in shock, and he's in the process of aiming his gun my way, but he's too slow. I've come at him out of nowhere, and I might not have skill, but I have a hammer, and surprise is my only advantage.

I slam my weapon right between his eyes with all the force I can muster, and when bone breaks, he collapses like a puppet dropped by the hand holding its strings. There's a dent between his brows now, where the claw of my hammer head went in, and when I rip it out, he makes a strange noise, shaking like a fish out of water. But as erratic as the bastard's acting, he is surely stronger and more capable than me, so I don't waste any time and bring the hammer down once more.

I'm in a daze, and right now, he's not human. He's a cockroach I need to exterminate. His limbs twitch a few more times, but once he stills, I freeze with the tool raised over my head, and only now sense sticky heat on my skin. I must be covered in blood.

I'm heaving as I look around at the five dead men, their blood coloring the snow like wine spilled on a pristine tablecloth. But then my attention turns to Cesar, still on his knees as if he hasn't even noticed me. He's rocking back and forth, making the tiniest little whines and covering his head.

I don't know what to do.

This must be some extreme PTSD or a panic attack of some sort.

I kneel right next to him, unsure if I should touch him right now, but I place my hands on his arms. "It's okay, it's okay, you're fine," I say, even though nothing is fine. This is a catastrophe. There's five dead men in our yard, my ankle's so numb I can barely feel it, and the one person I can trust acts as if I'm not there.

"Cesar, it's me, Eli. They're all dead, you're safe," I try, rubbing his shoulders, which are now covered by blood-soaked fabric. I should be disgusted. I should be afraid, but Cesar's safety takes precedence and I attempt to hug him.

Again, no reaction.

He's shaking like a terrified puppy, and dread creeps deeper into my heart. Because what if I can't wake him up from... whatever state this is? I'm not strong enough to carry him inside, I would have to drag him. At this rate, he might just freeze to death or fall seriously ill.

I'm so overwhelmed and out of my depth stupid tears form in my eyes. I rub them away because there's no time for feeling sorry for myself. I started the chain of events that led us both here.

"I love you?" I whisper with a heavy heart, looking into Cesar's vacant eye.

It's as though he's staring through me.

My heart shatters into a million ice shards.

I take a deep breath of air that smells of pine and blood, trying to think of something to help Cesar, other than my pathetic confessions. I remember that the guy who made Cesar fold to the ground said something to him. Instead of using his gun, he fiddled with some piece of paper.

On hands and knees I shuffle in the cold mud to reach the dead body. I don't have time to be frightened when

Cesar's life is on the line. The guy is still squeezing the small card in his cooling fingers. I rip it out, but of course, I'm so nervous, and my fingers tremble so much it falls. I grab it in panic to save it from soaking.

Something on this short list of sentences forced Cesar into the state he's in now, and I have to work out the solution to whatever mind game is still in progress. At the top of the card is a three-line list of words with no obvious connections, below it, a single sentence.

To end: 'Good dogs get their treats.'

My mouth dries, and I look up, taking in the dead bodies, and all the red stains on snow that used to be so pristine, but they offer no answers. The only clue I have is that ratty piece of paper, and when Cesar squeals, I turn on my knees to face him and read the last sentence out loud.

"Good dogs get their treats."

My tongue feels like a piece of wood, so very stiff in my mouth, but while Cesar remains in place, his shoulders relax and he lifts his head to glance my way.

Tears have cascaded down his cheek, washing away some of the blood left behind by the four kills he succeeded at before the final thug brought him to his knees. He's still not fully himself, but there's a person watching me now, and I almost bawl with relief.

But it's like he doesn't fully *see* me despite looking straight at me.

"Cesar? What is all of this about?" I ask, tucking the paper away as I crawl toward him.

He blinks, and this time, there seems to be more thought behind his glossy eye. "E—Eli?" he asks, as if he isn't sure he remembers my name correctly.

"Yes. Yes, me, Eli," I utter and cup his face to grab all his focus. His eye shuts, as if there was no greater relief than my touch, and he turns his face to lick my blood-stained palm.

"I'm your weapon…"

I gasp, my eyes growing wider. "No, no, no… I love you. That's what you're for. For my love. It's all okay, we'll work out whatever happened here."

The handsome face relaxes, and a low hum leaves Cesar's mouth as he pushes his face against my chest. The cold air stings my skin, but when I feel him *breathe me in*, heat spreads all over my body, all the way to the toes.

Surprised, I shuffle back toward the cabin, but then my back hits the lowest step, and he has me trapped, kissing his way up as if he needs closeness. "You are mine," he rasps and licks me through fabric.

"Y-yes. Yours," I utter, my heartbeat quickening. Dead bodies lie a few feet away, we're both stained with blood, and I should probably reject his touch, but I'm not reasonable when it comes to Cesar. And it's not just about his looks, or the way he takes care of me. I feel a spark between us that is irrational, rooted in the fury inside me that only he understands.

I want to be his.

Whatever he is. Whoever he is.

As he glides up the length of my body, he captures both of my wrists and brings them above my head. I shiver, stretching when he drags my chin up with his head, and then presses our mouths together in a shockingly chaste yet exciting kiss. No one before has ever had this kind of effect on me, and I doubt anyone else ever will.

We're like two sides of the same coin.

"You said however and whenever I want?" he rasps, meeting my gaze.

"Yes." I don't hesitate, because it's my biggest fucking turn-on to be desired like this. I plunged a hammer into a man's head, and he still wants me. My toes curl as I realize how much I'm into whatever he wants to do to me. I saw him kill four people, and I'm not afraid at all.

I spread my thighs, in a state of complete surrender, and he likes it. I can see it in the raw desire blooming on his features.

"Mine," he whispers and leans in for a kiss, his hands cradling my head while his tongue goes in deep, penetrating me as if he wants to show me I have no way out. But why would I ever want to run from someone who needs me so desperately?

I rock my body against his, using his knee to tease my growing cock, but I know we will not be making love for hours. Not in the cold mud. Raw sexual energy sparks in the air, and I am more than ready for it.

A gasp tears from my lips when Cesar flips me over, so I now face the porch, my elbows resting one step below it. There are only a couple of steps between us and the warmth of the cabin, but who needs comfort when I can be ravished by this beast of a man, right after he's saved my life from those strangers.

If this is what he needs now, a fuck after a kill, I'll give it to him.

I don't know if it's a kink, or if I'm just that much of a pleaser, but this is exactly how I want to be treated. He can bring me a cold compress and marshmallows later, but while we're having sex, there's nothing I crave more than to be *his* possession. I'm already hard as I offer myself to him, pushing back my ass and rubbing it against his groin.

Take me, I'm wordlessly saying, *use me. I'm your prey, so hunt me down and satisfy your hunger.*

He's quick and to the point about pulling my pants down. The air might be cold, but my face is on fire. We fuck around so much I always have lube on me, so I pass him the packet, panting against the step of the porch.

I'm happy to let him take his satisfaction inside my body, and know he's that bit more peaceful thanks to *me*.

He bites my shoulder blade through the top I'm wearing, but while it stings, there's a flash of pleasure in it too, and I lean into his touch listening to the quick slurp of lube. I know it'll happen very soon. I will have him inside, and it will burn, and I *will love it*.

"You need me," Cesar whispers, teasing my ear with his breath, but then his cock parts my ass cheeks, and I whine, pressing my face to the cold wood.

He's such a fucking stud. I knew he could break me in half even before I saw him kill four people, but he won't hurt me. I'm his precious possession. "Yes," I utter as he makes a quick jab with his hips, pushing his cockhead in.

There's some pain, but most of all, I feel relief. As if we've slotted back together after the horror laid bare in our yard. He grabs my sides with such possessiveness my heart melts a little.

All my life, this is all I've wanted. To belong with someone.

"I need you," I add, unashamed of my desperation, and I spread my legs as wide as the jeans pooled at my knees allow. "Come inside."

The sound coming from his lips sounds almost like an expression of pain, but I understand, because when he drills his way inside me, embedding his long cock in my hole, I too can't hold my voice in. My cry is loud, effortless, and I don't even try to bother stifling it, because anyone who could possibly overhear it lies dead.

"And I need you. I'm yours completely," he whispers in a trembling voice and wraps me in a tight embrace, with one of those wonderful hands resting on my throat.

Each thrust takes my breath away, and while the friction feels almost like too much, I don't want him to stop, or even slow down. I want him to jab into me just like this until he's so spent he can barely move.

I want to be his peace. His solace. This scary wolf's beloved bitch.

Is it messed up? Sure, but I don't care. No one needs to know. No one would understand this murder bond we share anyway. For any outsider, we're two monsters mating like we're animals.

His dick feels so good inside me. I love being under Cesar. I become Jello, my thighs tremble at each of his thrusts, and my own cock pulses with heat and desire to be touched. But my man comes first. That's the natural order of things, and he is not holding back.

Teeth and lips trail over my neck, nipping, licking, sucking, until I'm breathless with need, but then he's coming, and blood rushes to my face when I feel him pulse inside me.

There has never been a better feeling.

Nothing can compare.

"You smell so good," Cesar mumbles as his cock retreats from my body with a wet slap that makes me rock against him. When he licks my nape, it's like a spark of lust going straight to my cock, and I feel so needy I'm making incoherent, whiny noises.

"Please...?" I utter helplessly. I could jerk off, yet it feels like he's in full control of me and has to allow it. My face is hot, my bloodstained hands are sweaty, and I'm in a whole new universe with Cesar.

But instead of granting me permission, or even sucking me off like he sometimes does, Cesar pulls me into his arms and gets up. My dick is still hard, I'm probably dripping his cum, and he carries me like that to the cabin, leaving the massacre behind.

I don't even look back at the carnage, focused on Cesar's flushed face instead.

I have never seen a more handsome monster.

CHAPTER 15

CESAR

I DREAD TO IMAGINE what could have happened if it hadn't been for Eli.

My mind's still fuzzy, like a dark labyrinth around my soul, but the windows are now cracked wide enough to let in daylight and guide me to my sweet, beautiful companion.

With Sullivan dead, I'd thought myself untouchable, free of a leash that hung over me like a noose, but as it turns out, my former master put safeguards in place and entrusted *the words* to Lyle. I don't remember them. The first few—yes—but once I'm past a threshold, parts of me disappear, turned off, as if my body was a building and the person saying the long phrase held the power to turn off the lights.

I might be fearless, but when that happens, I'm scared like the child I was when that reaction was first instilled in me. With *the words*, Lyle had the power to make me obey and even die, but Eli freed me. Eli pulled me back to the surface. How can I ever repay him?

Our bodies are steaming hot as I push past the door and enter the cabin with my pants pooling at my ankles. I gravitate toward the couch, eager to give him the comfort he surely needs. I have so much mess to deal with, but first, I shall take care of Eli, give him pleasure and leave him to rest under a blanket.

He's wonderful.

I don't deserve him.

He has eyes only for me. Parts of what happened right after he pulled me out are vague, as if I'm not myself, but the attack dog I was forged into.

As through fog, I remember the word love being repeated. Another thing I don't deserve but which he gives me so freely.

I don't know what Eli's done, but there's lots of blood drying on him, and a hammer laid next to Lyle's smashed-in head. He's no experienced killer, yet he did that. For me.

And now I have him in my arms. So vulnerable, half naked, his cock still hard, his face red. I'm horny again just looking at him when I think that he's got my cum inside him. I'm calming down, getting back to myself, but the beast is still there as I change the angle of my arm so I can reach his hole with my fingers. So slippery and available.

Mine.

Mine. Mine. Mine.

My cock was already softening, but somewhere between the door and the couch, my brain started buzzing with desire, as if I haven't just come. It's insane. *He* is making me insane, but who the fuck cares? I want him, and he told me I should take him whenever I need to.

Right now, I most definitely do.

There's a rug in front of the log burner, and when I step on it, it becomes clear I don't want to wait a moment longer.

Eli holds on to me with more force when I lower both of us to the floor. I only let go of him when I'm sure it's safe, and he whines, rolling his hips impatiently. His cock is so hard it might burst at any moment, balls like two weights, and when he spreads his legs, the slick hole between his buttocks beckons me closer. It's swollen from our fuck, ripe, tender, and I want to be inside it again like I've never wanted anything in my life.

Maybe it's the effects of my trance, the adrenaline and shock of being taken down with such ease, but I want to fill Eli with my DNA, and turn him into a trembling, moaning mess who can't live without me.

He glances over his shoulder, but I can't wait and pull him to my chest as we lie almost flat, his face in the rug.

He makes that little whine I love so much. Like he's the cute slinky fox to my wolf. He turns his head enough to meet my eye, his own widening when I press my cock into his crack.

"Again?" he whispers, but rocks back like a good boy, and my dick breaches his cum-slicked channel with ease.

"Ohh fuck," I mumble when Eli's legs slide all the way apart, and I lie flat on top of him.

Eli wiggles under me, and while he might have taken down Lyle, he's no match for me, and will be staying where I want him unless I let him out. Which isn't soon, because his ass feels so good.

"Yes. Take what you need," he mumbles, half-lucid. "It's so thick…"

I've had pliant sex partners before, but Eli is something else. He gives himself completely. His body is mine. He might have taken over the reins from Sullivan, but the relationship between us is nothing like the one I had with my previous master. I used to be the dog beaten into obedience. Now I'm the domesticated wolf who pulls the leash a little too hard, yet gets petted nonetheless.

The rush in my head is impossible to describe. All I know is that I need *more*. Harder. Faster.

I drag his pants down, until one leg is off, and he can spread his thighs wider, and then wrap him in my arms as tightly as I can, until his back feels like an integral part of my own body. He smells like life. Like the summer, and spring. Like freedom. It's indescribable, and being inside his body—incomparable to fucking any other man in my past.

He's my North Star. The only person who matters, and I'll fuck him until he can't imagine a life without me.

"Do you like that? Stretching your tight hole so it's perfect for my dick," I rasp and bite his ear. "I can't help myself, I need to leave another load inside you."

His moans are perfection every time I slap my hips hard against his ass. "Yes. Oh fuck. Breed me whenever, I'm your bitch, and you're my wolf."

I'm melting. My brain is no longer on, because all I know is the tightness of his ass, the soft warmth of his body, and that scent, which I want to only ever sense in combination with mine.

"Then take it. Take my cock," I growl, holding him while my hips work, thrusting into him rapidly. The world's falling out of focus, but I don't care as long as I'm allowed on top of him, inside him.

We really are like two animals, and I react to every twitch, every moan he makes, rewarding him with kisses and nips he's so very eager for.

"Fuck. You're hitting the right spot," Eli whines. "Feel that?" he asks and I gasp when he squeezes the muscles in his ass around me several times, sucking me in, hugging me again and again until I can't help it and let him milk me dry.

I fall, jabbing my hips into him as ecstasy swirls inside me, squeezing my balls until they're so empty they ache. Fuck, how I want him. How very badly I need him with me now, and even as my cock is too sensitive to keep up with the fucking, a part of me wants to keep going while he goes wild.

I settle on top of him, catching my breath, completely pumped out. In the glow of my easing arousal, I slide my hands up the sides of his body, just enjoying how his hair smells of my shampoo, and how much warmth the nearby fire gives us.

"I love feeling it inside me," Eli confesses in a whisper, gently wiggling his ass.

I grin and push my face into the crook of his neck, kissing his skin. This time, my dick retreats on its own, softening, and I follow the fragrant trail of sweat down Eli's back, rubbing my face against him while he moans, still not satisfied.

I wish I could give him more, and I'm half of the mind to fuck him with my fingers next. But when I kneel behind him and see what a delicious sight he makes with cum pooling between the cheeks of his ass, a frenzy makes me drag his hips up and dive right in.

He's salty, musky, and absolutely delicious when his body goes limp in front of me.

"Oh my God. Oh *my* God. Fuck you're good at this," Eli says between one gasp and another, not making a single protest about the new position.

I can see his dick now, and the trail of pre-cum it left on the rug. It's like a ripe fruit, so I grab it as I get back to eating his ass, licking it up. Eli's little wiggles spur me on as he tries to fuck my hand, needy like a cat in heat.

I love the earthy taste of his body, but the texture of that delicate flesh is somehow even better, so I give it my all, caressing him while I stroke his dick. His hole tightens around the tip of my tongue, and then I feel him coming, and even the scent of his body changes when charges of bliss pulse through him in rapid succession.

Still, I only stop eating him when he's slumped on the rug, his batteries drained even more than mine.

Rolling to my back, I stare at the ceiling and find Eli's warm hand. "Thank you..."

He shifts to his side to lay close to me, a beautiful mess of a man only I can handle.

"Cesar... I have so many questions, but no energy to ask them." Eli kisses my shoulder with his eyes closed, but that's not enough for me, so I pull him closer, until his gray head rests on my chest.

"Yeah. I'm all pumped out too," I mumble, stretching on the rug.

"I need to know if we're safe for now or if we should expect more 'guests'."

I roll my head left and right. "Don't think so. At least not immediately, but if they don't make contact for too long, there might be someone new coming. I think we should leave tomorrow."

"And who the fuck were they? Who did I kill?" he lowers his voice as if the ghosts of the men left outside could hear him.

I shrug. "Ah, Lyle, Sullivan's personal security and an all-round dickhead. Sorry you had to be involved, lamb."

"Funny you'd call me that, *wolf*. I know a tiny bit about your past, but the way you dealt with them was still… very proficient. You didn't hesitate. What did Lyle do to you at the end?" Eli opens his eyes, his brows drawn, but even though he acknowledges what he saw, he still strokes my side as if I'm *his* pet wolf.

His touch is the only thing keeping me from freezing over, because of course my past has caught up with me. It couldn't just stay where the past should like I wanted, and now… now he'll find out all I've kept hidden. Because what's the point of coming up with another lie? Especially after he's been an open book to me about everything.

My hope is that he wants me too much to leave.

"You… weren't meant to see any of that." He opens his mouth, but I shush him with a gesture and sigh, focusing on the patterns in the wood making up the ceiling. "I wanted to have a fresh start too. A new life, where my past did not matter, but I did lie to you. I'm sorry."

"You're not an ex-soldier?" he guesses with a sigh. "When you spoke to them at first, I worried you just caught me for them, and enjoyed your time waiting until they come collect me. But your loyalty was to me. Why?"

I'm breathless when I glance his way, my heart beating so fast it's giving me vertigo. "I would never! Of course I'm loyal to you. My life belongs to you," I mumble, flinching when he strokes my stomach, as if wanting to appease me. But I'm hurt. Of course I am, because he is my whole world now.

He watches me with such softness in his gray eyes. No one's ever showered me with tenderness the way he does. "I felt that. My gut told me to stay. But I need to know what's going on. What is this code? What happened to you?" He reaches all the way to the pocket of his jeans, and I miss his touch for the three seconds he's away. He shows me the piece of paper where Lyle had the key to my obedience written down, and I close my eyes, not wanting to see it.

Spiders crawl all over my body, and I roll to my side, facing away from him as I try to rein in the panic growing inside. I know it's not safe to really show him how wary I am of those few lines of text, but their proximity is like a dagger held to my throat and about to cut through skin.

"He trained me to react to those words from very early on. I was six, maybe seven," I mumble. "He was relentless."

"Who? Sullivan? Cesar, look at me, please."

I swallow with worry, but how can I resist his plea? Moments later, I'm peeking at him above my shoulder. "Yes, him. I grew up in his home. My parents paid off their debts by giving me to him. Just left me there one Christmas, like that unwanted gift you pass on to someone else."

Eli opens the wood burner and throws the paper inside. He couldn't have had time to memorize the command. Even though I'm a dangerous monster, he doesn't want to control me.

"You're not unwanted," he says, and sits up, legs crossed.

He sounds so sincere and honest I can barely resist and roll to my back again, seeking his hand. "I want you too. You killed him, so I owe you everything."

Eli squeezes my hand, looking straight into my eye. "If you owe me everything, you owe me the truth. Who are you, Cesar?"

Truth rolls out of my mouth, because he demands it. "I used to be Sullivan's bodyguard before Lyle. I am also his best killer. He had me trained for it since I was five. But now I'm retired. I was always meant to retire once my tattoo is finished," I tell him and move my fingers down my body. "He picked a design to stand for my best job of the year. But for the past two… he refused, because I lost my eye, and he sidelined me. So I was still bound to him, constantly on call, with the exception of Fridays," I tell him.

Eli soaks it all in like a sponge, not even blinking. "You're so… proficient. Why didn't you just kill him once you grew up?"

"I wanted to, but he had *the words* to stop me. He also told me an implant was placed on my heart, and he could use it to stop it remotely," I say, tracing the scar on my chest. When Eli's eyes widen, I clear my throat and shrug. "I used to believe that when I was younger. Now… I no longer do, but a part of me still wonders *what if*. That's why I'm so unsettled during storms. It messes with my head. I was only ten when I had a surgery and woke up with this massive scar. Over the years of working for Sullivan, my forced loyalty to him was so built in I just… couldn't overcome it, even if it's unreasonable. He had a power over me."

"And yet you didn't want to avenge him for what I did?"

My body relaxes and I press his hand to my chest, because this is so much easier to talk about. I want my whole life to revolve around him. "No. I would be adrift without Sullivan letting me go, but you removed him and I decided to give back. Help you escape. Now I know I don't want to leave your side."

He smiles at me, and it's as if the warmth of the wood burner becomes stronger, enveloping me so pleasantly. "Without your help I would have already been in prison if not shot. We only have each other, but that's more than enough for me. I meant it when I said it. I love you. I know it. You're everything I need."

My chest tightens, and I shift, pushing my head against his chest. I might not be enough, but I'll still do my best so he never regrets being with me. "I... can't give you that in return, I'm sorry. I can't feel love. I'm empty. It's what my training did to me. But I will always stand by you, take care of you, and I will be the best boyfriend you could have. Promise."

Will that be enough?

Is this an exchange he can accept, or is this lovely thing between us over?

He watches me in silence for a while, and I wish I could know what's going on in his head. I dread the outcome once he opens his mouth.

"That's ridiculous. No one can take that away from you, and you've been nothing but loving to me."

I frown, because what does he know about what I've been through, but I'm tired and don't want to argue. "I like being with you."

Eli leans close and bumps his shoulder against mine. "I will prove to you that you're capable of love. Even if it takes me a lifetime."

He's so sweet. Sweeter than I deserve, but before I can think his words through, I notice his ankle and sit right up.

It's swollen.

"No... what...? What happened? Was that me?" I ask as guilt trails down my body.

Eli shakes his head. "Ah. That. Price of freedom, I guess. I crawled out through the window in the attic, and then slid down the roof John Wick style to surprise Lyle with my hammer. There wasn't much time to think it through, because he had you at gunpoint, but... yeah, I fell on the bad ankle."

Unbelievable.

"I told you to take it easy," I mumble, but the truth is what's done is done. Neither of us can reverse time, so I shake my head and meet his gaze. "Fine. We'll ice it, and then you'll rest, and I get rid of the bodies. We will be driving off tomorrow."

Eli looks at the Christmas tree with longing. "I did hope we'd be here a little longer. Oh well, goodbye Christmas cabin where I met the love of my life."

He winks at me, and my heart melts a little.

Chapter 16

Cesar

Within twenty-four hours, we head north, while the plume of smoke rising from the cabin paints dark swirls on the bright sky. The fire would not go unnoticed, and someone would check the place eventually, but the damp, snowy woods were a fitting pyre for Lyle and co.

I arranged the bodies in a way suggesting they all died fighting each other, even left most of their weapons behind, alongside the SUV I stole almost two weeks back. Sullivan's organization might now be up in flames as different players fight to fill the power vacuum, but we only have so much time until they realize five men and two vehicles have been lost. Until then, the bright yellow SUV will work well for our needs. It has heated seats at the front, so Eli can be nice and cozy during his naps.

It was adorable that he insisted on helping with the bodies, but I had to be stern with him. He's hurt his ankle *again*, and he's not allowed to strain himself until we know what's going on with it. I'm still in awe of him when I think he jumped off a roof for me and smashed Lyle's head in with a hammer. I don't know if I deserve that much affection, but I'm still gonna take it.

We're both sad to lose our safe haven, but I chose to take a bit of it with us and cut some of the decorated branches off our Christmas tree. I've placed them in the back seat, and attached several to the ceiling to create a place where Eli can relax during our way north.

That man's like a cat. If he can take a nap, he will, and he's asleep even now. We've had barely two weeks together, but I think his face has already filled in a little, and while still slender, he looks healthier now, less pale. I will make sure he always has what he needs.

And that includes medical attention.

It takes me a while to find a provider that's right for us, and so does moving north using smaller roads, where we're less likely to be flagged by automated systems, but eventually I arrive at the far end of a parking lot behind a supermarket and stop close to the mobile clinic the size of a shipping container. The outer lamp is already off, but I exhale with relief at the sight of the car parked next to it. I was worried we might arrive too late, but the attending physician must still be in.

"Lamb, wake up," I say and squeeze his shoulder, before making sure the disposable mask he's wearing, to minimize the chance of being recognized, is not out of place.

The way he blinks at me, so sleepy... I just want to squish his cheeks and eat him up. I'm glad he lets me fuck him bare, because I couldn't stand anything between us.

One yawn later, Eli is able to speak. "Hm? Where are we? Snacks?"

Even the way he says that last word is precious.

Snacks.

But this is not the time to feed my addiction to him, so I comb his hair with my fingers. "Your ankle needs an X-Ray. Let's get you inside," I say and open the door.

Eli's eyes widen. "What? I can't go to a hospital. I'll get arrested."

The red woolen hat hides his gray hair, one of the features that would make him recognizable. I also chose red for when we were at the cabin, so I could spot him in the woods with ease. Now that we're back among people, he might need a hat that stands out less. But right now, there are other concerns.

"That's why we're not in a hospital," I say and approach his side of the car. His ankle is still terribly swollen, and I'd be a lousy partner if I left him to suffer, and maybe even end up with permanent damage.

As soon as Eli tries to get out, I shoulder as much of his weight as I can without carrying him.

"What is this place?" he asks, looking around, but it's late, and he won't be able to see much beyond the faint glow of the lamps in the parking lot.

"Middle of nowhere. We had to make a little detour, but I can pull some strings here," I tell him. When I see the way he's limping, I can't help myself after all. I lean down to push my arm under the backs of his knees, then lift him up on my way to the clinic.

We're halfway there when a woman with short dark hair steps out with a key in hand. She stalls, takes us in, then shakes her head.

"I'm so sorry, we're closed. Besides, it's only me now. The doctor already left. I can provide you with the address of the nearest Emergency Department."

"You're an X-ray technician. That's all we need," I say, continuing on my way. She takes a step back inside, squeezing one hand on the door handle, as if she feared I'm here to rob her.

"I'm sorry but how do you—"

She doesn't know me, but I was one of the men who beat up her husband to force him into paying his debt to Mr. Sullivan. And I know the way she ended up obtaining the money was far from legal.

I did not pick this particular place just because of there not being that many cameras around.

"I worked with the man your husband borrowed money from, and I know how you covered his debts," I tell her simply, because all I want is the X-ray. I'm not here to mess up her evening.

She straightens, and I can see her going pale. I wouldn't want to meet me at night either.

"Can I never move on from this? I thought it all ended with that Festive Fugitive guy. Sullivan's dead. What do you want?" The jingle of keys in her hand tells me they're trembling even though she's holding them behind her back.

"As I said, I just need to know if his bones are whole," I say, approaching her calmly. "I will pay you for your trouble. All I want is discretion."

She takes a deep breath, reassessing the situation with a frown. Her gaze lands on Eli's leg. "Okay, let's just be quick."

"I'm so sorry," Eli mumbles through his mask, but she shakes her head and leads us in.

"Don't tell me anything. I don't need to know why you can't go to a normal hospital, or what your names are," she says as we step into the tight space featuring a desk, chairs, lots of storage, and the mobile X-ray unit at the back. Considering the size of the trailer, I can only assume there's another room that can be entered from the back, but just like her, I don't need to know everything.

The procedure goes very swiftly after that. Eli's ankle is whole, and the swelling is due to a bad sprain. Nurse Patch recommends we purchase a support brace, and I already know that will be the first thing we do once we're out of here. The supermarket should stock them, actually. If it's closed, I can probably break in without much trouble. Maybe even get Eli snacks while I'm there.

We're about to leave when Eli stops both me and the nurse. "Wait. While we're here, real quick, could we please take an X-ray of his chest?" He pats my shoulder.

After a stunned second, I know what this is about, and while he's being thoughtful, I break out in a cold sweat.

"Why?" the nurse asks, picking on the reindeer pin attached to her scrubs, but she must have realized this unexpected visit will be over faster if she does what we want her to, so she approaches the machine to shift things around.

For a moment, I say nothing, eyeing Eli with an uncertainty I rarely feel. "There is no need," I whisper.

"You'd finally be certain." He strokes my face, his eyes so soft and full of compassion I could drown in them. "And if it is there, you'd know to extract it in the future. If it's not, you'd be free."

I know he's right, that this has been going for far too long, but agreeing feels like jumping into a dark cavern without anything to keep me safe. My brain is pounding as if it's grown too big for my head, and I can't think. "Sullivan will know. He will punish me," I tell him in a low voice and lick the sweat from above my lip.

Eli's cold fingers trail over my hand. "Sullivan's gone, Wolf. You're free to do as you wish." He's probably not using my name in case the nurse is eavesdropping, but it feels so tender and personal when he calls me that. He knows I'm dangerous, yet has no fear around me. He trusts me. Cherishes me. Wants what's best for me.

And when he looks at me from behind the mask that hides his identity, I know I can't stand disappointing him.

He's the one I live for now.

"So... you want me to do it?"

Eli nods. "If not for yourself, would you please do it for me? I need to know what we're up against."

'We'. As if my problems are his to handle. As if he's the one who ought to take care of me, not the other way around. A part of me wants to correct him, but he squeezes my hand, and it's clear to me then that my obedience will make him happy.

How can I refuse?

There's a siren ringing in my ears, like a tornado warning, when I stand in place, about to risk that my body is in fact rigged and self-destructs. But I've been through so much worse, so when the nurse steps away, I lock eyes with my sweet lamb, who gives me an encouraging smile.

It's hard to breathe when anticipation twists my ligaments as if I'm a human-sized salami, but then the apparatus beeps and—

"We're done" the woman says, and I stare at her, unsure if it really is over.

Nothing's happened.

I'm still whole. And Sullivan's dead and can no longer reach me.

"Anything in there?" Eli asks, limping to the nurse's side. "Any metal in or around his heart?"

I dress in my coat while she takes her time, but once the photo is mounted on the bright screen, one thing is as obvious as the fact that I would rather die than disappoint Eli—there's nothing of note inside my chest.

No implants. No bombs. No remotely-activated poison vials.

I'm all flesh and bone, like most people who don't share my history.

"I don't know what the hell you two are looking for, but I don't see it," she says and frowns at us.

I take a deep breath, but I'm unable to speak anyway. Eli steps in without hesitation. "We are so grateful for the help, and we'll pay, but could you please give us a moment here? After that, you'll never see us again."

The nurse glances around the expensive equipment but must have figured we're not about to steal or sabotage any of it, because she eventually nods.

"Five minutes. Tops," she says and leaves.

As soon as she's out, Eli turns to me and strokes my arm. "See? It's okay. You're free."

It doesn't seem real, and the tiny Christmas tree perched on top of the nearby cabinet makes the whole thing even more ridiculous.

Then again, maybe it's me who's the joke, believing Sullivan's lies after his death?

"I'm free," I repeat, tightening my hands on Eli's.

His smile is pure sunshine, and I find myself on my knees, face pressed to his stomach as I hug him. He's so quick to stroke my head. He doesn't judge my weakness or despise it. He's the antithesis of what I've been taught my whole life.

That anyone who learns who I truly am will leave me.

That tears are pathetic.

That only physical strength matters.

That friendships are defects.

That anyone who claims to care about me is lying.

"It's okay. Take your time. I know this must be a very hard revelation. I can't imagine he had you cut up like that just to keep you frightened. You were only a child." Eli goes down to his knees with me and hugs me, stroking my scar through my sweater. His scent is so soothing. I wouldn't need to see or hear him to recognize him.

I should scold him for risking his ankle again, but that's okay. I'll pick him up and carry him straight to the car once I'm no longer on the verge of hyperventilating.

Such a strange feeling.

As if my chest is so full I can no longer breathe. It hurts. But I don't want it to end, as if deep down I'm aware that the pain proves I'm as human as anyone else.

"It was hard, growing up without a childhood," I whisper, meeting Eli's gaze. "I needed to do as I was told, or face the consequences. Nobody would give me slack just because I was a kid. When I tried to rebel, they... they did this to me. Just to lie to me, told me they could kill me even if I ran away." I put my hand over Eli's, right over my heart.

Eli sits his ass on the floor and pulls me closer. He's half my size, but I feel so safe in his arms. If I did have a destructive implant in my heart, I could give him the remote and know he'd never hurt me.

"I can't imagine what you've been through," he whispers against my temple. "I'm here for you."

He's so warm, sweet, fragrant. He's everything I want and need, so I hate the niggling feeling at the back of my mind that I don't deserve any of it. "I don't know if I can give you what you want. I'm sorry."

"It's okay, I'm getting everything I need. Though I can't imagine why you'd think you can't love. You're so tender with me." Eli leaves several soothing kisses on my face, and I arch toward him as if I'm someone who's spent their life underground and is only now seeing light for the first time.

"I killed my parents. That was a graduation of sorts. Once they were gone, I had no ties to my past. I watched their house burn and didn't even shed a single tear. That's not normal," I tell Eli, because someone like him surely can't imagine what it means to be me. "Sullivan patted me on the back after that. The one and only time I think he fully expressed his approval of me in any way. But I knew I was broken."

Eli is silent for a while as he looks into my eye. I'm wearing the fake one, but he knows which one is real. "Maybe they deserved it for leaving you in Sullivan's claws. I'm not sorry about the two people I killed. Does that make me a monster?"

Ridiculous.

"Of course not. But we're not the same."

He's about to answer, but that's when we both hear raised voices over the low hum of the generator keeping this place fed with electricity. I press my index finger to Eli's soft lips and rise, quietly approaching the door. When I first hear the nurse's voice, I'm convinced she's calling the cops, but moments later, another woman speaks up in a shrill tone.

"This is last month all over again! I knew you were doing something under the table. Who are those people, and why do they need to grease your palm to be seen after hours, huh?"

Fuck. Apparently, this isn't the first time Nurse Patch has drawn the suspicion of her colleagues, but I won't shoulder the fallout, and neither will Eli.

He's wanted, so the last thing we need is this nosy woman drawing attention to our presence.

I step outside, immediately shutting the door, and both Nurse Patch and a younger lady with blonde hair focus on me.

"And who are you?" she asks, showing me the phone she's holding. "If I press this button, the police will be here in minutes!"

Just great.

"Lady, you need to stop participating in the system like a gullible child," I improvise, but while she frowns at me, offended, there's interest in her gaze, so I continue. "The government secretly implants chips in the backs of our heads, and the only way to find out and *not be found* out is to check it beyond the system. Mrs. Patch is just doing me a favor, and I won't let you badmouth her!"

I'm a much better killer than an actor, but the new woman is gobbling it up.

Patch just watches me with dead eyes. "Yeah. He wouldn't leave unless I scanned him off the books."

The blonde wraps her arms on her chest and frowns. I brace myself for a slew of insults. "What... kind of chips? You know, my uncle has been complaining about an itch at the back of his head ever since he came out of the army."

I point at her and nod. "Exactly what I'm talking about. I'm a vet too, but the government surveillance continues!"

The woman glances at Patch. "Okay, fine, whatever, just go, but don't bring any of your friends here for this. We can't lose the contract for working here. We will talk about this tomorrow," she adds, opening her car. I watch her leave, and only once we can no longer see the back lights of her vehicle do I approach the nurse with a wad of cash.

"Thank you. We'll be out of your hair."

I go right back in, and before Eli can protest that he'll limp instead, I pick him up. It feels as if instead of weakening me, the conversation with him has only made me stronger.

He pulls down his mask as we walk away so I can see his smile. "That was pretty funny."

He always has a new compliment for me.

My urge to treat him is so strong I already have several ideas of how to do that.

Chapter 17

ELI

I've never napped this much in my life. Cesar's presence is so reassuring, my body so happily shuts down under a blanket while he drives us someplace only he knows.

"Snacks?" I ask when he wakes me up. I'm not that hungry, but it's becoming a joke between us, so I don't miss the opportunity to brighten his day. He needs it. The horrific things he's gone through have scarred him in ways deeper and more profound than any physical injuries he's endured. I'll do anything in my power to support him, even if I can't offer that much.

It's already dark, but as he leans over me, stroking the side of my head, I spot warm lights behind him. "Wakey, wakey. Time to treat ourselves to a nice time on Christmas Eve," he says, pointing at the large Christmas tree right outside our car window.

I smile at him, because it gets me all fuzzy inside that he's getting into the Christmas spirit. I want him to have that. So what if he's a killer? Maybe it's fucked up, but *life* is fucked up. Mine definitely is.

"You prepared something? Where are we?" I push off my blanket, trying to work out our new location.

He glances over his shoulder and smirks. "Prepared is too big of a word. But I think you deserve a break. Someone canceled their reservation last minute, and I snatched the room."

I open the car door and I finally see it.

Holly Falls Lodge and Spa spelled in elegant letters above a grand entrance to a sprawling building sat above a gorge. I can see it all quite clearly thanks to the opulent Christmas decorations sparkling with colorful lights.

And then I hear something else. I don't wait for Cesar to assist me and limp out to a barrier beyond which I hear the waterfall the resort was surely named after.

"Cesar! Come look at this!" I yell in excitement as the cool breeze hits my face and I inhale the fresh scent.

Which reminds me I should be wearing my mask, but there's no one here. Nobody to see me in the shadows as I marvel at the grand cascade of water illuminated with a golden-hued illumination. We're on the edge of a cliff overlooking the falls and the languid trail of the river, and while it's dark, so I can only see so much, I don't think I've ever seen anything more grand.

The sense of awe spreads through me, and I don't even flinch when Cesar puts the cloth mask on my face, hooking the straps behind my ears. "I've been here before," he tells me. "On a job, but this place is famous for their masked Christmas parties. We won't stand out too much."

I look back at him because right now, he's more awe worthy than the waterfall. "You thought of everything. I love you so much." I turn to him for a tight hug, amazed that I thought I'd ruined my life when I killed Sullivan, but instead it led me to Cesar, and he's rebuilding it brick by brick, into the most grandiose castle in existence.

He makes a small sound at the back of his throat, but after a moment's pause, his warm arms tighten around me until he's almost lifting me off the ground. I never knew safety could have a scent, but it's herbal, and dark, and I'm surrounded by it.

"I just want to make you happy. Do you... want to bring some of the branches from the cabin with us?" he asks, gesturing at the car.

"No, I think they'll fare better in the car, and it will smell nice when we come back." I grab his hand. I know it will make us stand out more, but who is going to think the Festive Fugitive has gotten himself a boyfriend in two weeks?

The building's dark wooden exterior is outlined with warm white string lights that trace the rooflines and gables, glowing against the night sky. The windows glow like golden panels, inviting us in, and I can't wait to find out what feast awaits us—

"Are you sure we can afford this?" I glance at Cesar as we approach the glass door. I can already see the towering Christmas tree by the reception area, topped by a golden star and decorated in classic colors of red and green.

This place is fancy, like a hotel for the rich in one of those feel-good Christmas movies, and as we approach the door, I imagine we are the main characters of a rom-com, and this is when my man will reveal that he can surround me with mind-blowing luxury, and that I will never have to worry about money again.

"Quite sure," he says, grinning at me, but his gaze drifts off when the automatic doors open and a tall man in a burgundy suit and wooden mask depicting a stylized reindeer muzzle steps out, ranting on his phone. I've never owned clothing that fine. Maybe, I could get something of that quality for my wedding, but that's about it.

"Is this my *Pretty Woman* moment? Next thing I know, you'll be buying me a suit like that guy's," I laugh and lead the way in, though Cesar is instantly alarmed and puts his arm around me to secure my wobbly walk. He got me a simple brace and pain meds, so I'm not even hurting, but that doesn't mean he takes care of me any less than before. I'm quite certain that if he didn't want to be more discreet, he would be carrying me all the way to my room.

The foyer's an upscale version of a lodge, with a floor of smooth stone, and the faint scent of winter berries hanging in the air as the guests socialize, have drinks by tables set up all over the area, or read.

Not everyone is masked, but Cesar and I are the worst-dressed people in the lobby. I fear everyone might be judging us, but my man approaches the reception as if he truly belongs here.

As he sorts out the details of our stay, I look around this festive heaven. It's a mix of luxury and rustic elements. Elegant armchairs upholstered with plaid fabric stand in front of a fireplace, and a deer trophy overlooks the men having drinks there. I can't wait to see our room, but I hope it will have a few Christmas decorations too.

I can almost forget that I'm a wanted criminal.

Tonight it's just me and my boyfriend who seems to have a bottomless bank account.

I stand by a wooden pillar, trying not to draw attention to myself, but a part of me still worries someone might recognize me by the shape of my eyes, so it's a relief when Cesar grabs my hand and leads me to the elevator.

Our room is on the top floor, and when I step in, the amount of space shocks me.

Just like downstairs, the furnishings are simple in form but luxurious. The bed is massive. The coffee table is made from a slab of raw wood. Two armchairs face our very own fireplace, and the TV mounted on the wall is larger than any I've ever owned myself.

I feel like a beggar invited to a palace.

"You know what? If the cops get me after this, I would have still felt that at least I *lived.*" My heart beats faster when I spot a Christmas tree by the large balcony door and I now realize that we are not only about to enjoy Christmas Eve at this incredible place. This is where we will also welcome Christmas *Day.*

I might be the happiest fugitive who ever lived.

I'm shocked to discover we have a balcony overlooking the falls, which I will be able to admire first thing in the morning, and the bathroom features a tub with water jets.

"Here, let me help you," Cesar says, pushing me onto the bed, then removing my boots.

"I'm really getting the princess treatment here. Thank you so much." I stroke his hair as my heart melts. I don't know what I've done to deserve him. When he kneels and puts his head in my lap, I'm terrified our happiness might come to an end at any moment, if somebody does recognize us, or if Cesar decides I am not in fact worth all this hassle. But I want to trust him with my heart, and with my body, and soon enough, my fears quiet down.

We've ordered a ridiculous amount of food from a menu that doesn't contain a price list, but at this point I am in for the ride. Who am I to question the contents of my man's wallet? If he wants to treat me, I'll let him.

I turn on the TV and start skipping through news channels as I stuff my mouth with a piece of cranberry pie with some alcohol in it. I hope *not* to find anything about the Festive Fugitive. It's been over two weeks, and there's a chance interest in me has died down in favor of exploring the depths of depravity discovered in Sullivan's basement. Cesar has fed me titbits of 'positive' information about the case, like people siding with me as the public opinion dissected my father's legal case against Sullivan, or speculation that Sullivan tortured me, and I just lost it in an act of revenge. Which is not untrue.

The reveal of my sexuality has apparently stirred up the public's interest in me, causing some people to speculate that I was Sullivan's sugar baby, or something. Cesar didn't want to show me most of those, but he did treat me to some funny memes about how I 'slay'. I also rather enjoyed the disses thrown at Spencer who decided to have his five minutes of fame on the back of my infamy. His other exes came out of the woodwork to spill all about how shitty of a boyfriend he was.

I never wanted my face all over the news, so I'm glad when instead of yet more segments about the chase, I see lovely videos from Christmas markets all around the world. I'm about to turn to some music channel when a familiar face appears on the screen.

It's my fucking *aunt*.

Despite it being such a happy season, she's in black, as if she's intent on expressing to the whole nation just how sad she is over my crimes. She's grown out her hair since I last saw her, and I'm happy the new fluffy hairstyle doesn't suit her.

She and the reporter are exchanging the usual set of questions and answers.

How does the family feel about this?

Does the situation affect how they're spending the holidays?

Does she have anything to say to her nephew, if he's watching? That, obviously, is *turn yourself in.*

Fat fucking chance.

But as unpleasant as it is to see her again, when my aunt starts to outright lie about our past relationship, my brain stews inside my skull.

"Yes, a year ago, we were still letting him stay with us, but he's always had anger issues, and we worried about our kids. But in the end, he just chose to disappear. He's very... troubled."

"Anger issues?" I yell, getting up so fast I almost spill my delicious mulled wine. "I can fucking show her anger issues! You know what she did? Her and her fucking husband used me for a year in their house like some fucking Cinderella just so I had a place to sleep. And that was in their garage by the way. I cooked, cleaned, served as a nanny, a chauffeur for their kids, their delivery boy, dogwalker, and everything you can damn imagine. And then they *kicked me out* right before Christmas last year because they wanted to invite *other* family over and needed the space!"

Cesar sighs and pulls me close. I'm like a kitten trying to get away from its owner's tight embrace, but I can't help being upset that another person is smearing my name in public.

"We could wait and take our revenge next Christmas," Cesar says with a soft rasp. "Have someone seduce her husband, set fire to the house..."

I take a deep breath as I watch him, my heart beating faster. He's always in my corner. "You know what? If I'm not dead or in prison by next year, maybe we fucking should. Because there's just no justice in the world otherwise."

He rolls on top of me and holds his weight with those freakishly strong arms as I take a sip of the mulled wine. "I will be all the justice you need. The world is cruel, people are petty, but you can count on me. Always."

I try to put the glass away, and when I can't reach the nightstand, he notices, of course, and helps me. I arch up to kiss his lips. Maybe I'm being love-bombed, but if so, then I'm doing it in return. I believe every word he says and they're tastier than the wine.

"I can see a world like that. Just the two of us," I whisper, shocked at how quickly he's calmed me down. I didn't even need to throw a lamp against the wall.

Cesar grins, kisses my lips, then places his palm on my chest before trailing it down my body. "That's it. I like that I have this effect on you, lamb."

I love when he calls me that. Like I no longer have the weight of the world on my shoulders, but I can trust someone else will herd me to safety. And there's no one I want more with me in this fresh-smelling soft bedding than Cesar.

"It's very easy for you to divert my attention." I'm so reactive to him. I love him for his personality traits, but wow, his body is something else, and whenever he's close, it feels as if his pheromones invade my brain until I can think of nothing but him naked.

"Pretty sure you're in need of a distraction now," Cesar tells me, lowering the fly of my pants. Despite his touch heading there, I didn't quite expect *that*, and I melt into the bed as anticipation comes to the surface like bubbles of air.

I bite my lip, watching him in awe. My beautiful beast rises off the bed, and I gasp when in one strong move he drags me to the edge of the bed by the legs, and then slides off my pants. "Nothing would relax me more." I'm pretty sure I know what he wants, but I'd go with whatever.

When Cesar kneels on the floor between my spread legs, my dick is already so hard it needs to be released as soon as possible, and I have to stop myself from reaching down to massage the bulge at the front of my underwear. The cotton's already damp in one spot, and I smile, noticing Cesar sees it too.

"I see a part of you is very stiff. Could do with a relaxing massage," he says, trailing his fingers along my inner thighs in a touch so featherlight, I can barely believe his hands are there.

When I do nothing to stop him, Cesar removes my underwear, then shuts his eyes and leans forward, cradling my cock in one hand as he flattens his tongue against its underside and licks me from base to tip. Electricity jolts up my body, making me arch up from the mattress, but he doesn't stop, and just as I'm about to reach the peak of my want, that wet, soft mouth opens up around my sensitive glans.

I let out a moan and give in to the ecstatic sensation. He's so good to me. And really does take away all my worries. Cesar's tongue is so attentive, and when I slide my hand into his short hair to pet him, he lets out a happy murmur that resonates all the way up my dick.

"So good, Cesar, so good..."

He doesn't bother saying anything back, just slides his arms around each of my bare thighs, as if he needs to hold me in place, and swallows me—first halfway then whole. I'm in fucking heaven, and only his magical doppelganger fucking my ass at the same time could have made this better.

My fingers weave through his hair, and while I don't intend to take the reins, he does react to the gentle touch, changing his pace and the angle at which he holds me in his mouth whenever I as much as twitch.

No one has ever been so attentive to my needs before, but while he's setting a new standard, I know he's right when he says I deserve this kind of care. My exes have taken me for granted, but not Cesar. Cesar sees me as this precious creature, and I want to let him.

He takes his time with me, making me forget any past boyfriends, or my stupid aunt, or the times I've killed. All trouble dissolves into nothingness.

"D-do you... want...?" I utter. I'm on the verge of orgasm, and it's hard to communicate with this tension building inside me, but if he wants my body in any other way before I come, I'm giving him the chance.

I look down in time to see him pull up and speak with my damp cock pressed to his moving lips, as if he were praying at my altar. "No, I want to wait. Whet my appetite for later," he says, his real eye a glinting light shining at me from behind the curtain of lashes. The artificial one seems dim in comparison, a pale echo of the real thing. I'm overcome by the need to let him do as he pleases and moan when he downs me again, sucking in a rhythm that has me twitching.

My balls tighten, I don't control the volume of my moans, and I fall back into the silky sheets. When Cesar slides his fingers to one of my feet and caresses my toe, I lose it.

I tighten my fingers in his hair, and come with such surprising intensity, my body trembles. I shut my eyes but still see a reflection of Cesar at the back of my eyelid. He's the man who pleasures me wanting nothing in return. I've always been anxious to give back, but he lets me relax and enjoy the ride.

I'm still panting and making little involuntary whimpers at each of his licks to my oversensitive cock. Never before him did I feel with a man that I could accept what was freely given, like I deserved it. But he is so devoted I can believe him. Believe that I am enough.

As I come down from my high, he climbs my body, eventually stretching alongside me, lips pressed to my forehead. "That's it, Lamb, relax. I've got you."

I press my face against his neck to hide the tears gathering under my eyelids. He might be claiming he can't love, that what he's been through killed the feeling inside him, but I've never felt so appreciated and cared for.

Safety. Trust. Affection. Throw in a grenade of lust, and isn't that love? How can he not see that he already gives me everything I could ever need?

It takes me a while to find my voice as I hug his sturdy chest. "You sure you want to wait?" I ask, nudging his cock through his jeans with my thigh. "My body is yours after all..."

Cesar's eye flickers, but he pulls his hips away. "Dessert should always come last. But what about you? Can I make your evening any better right now?" he asks, rubbing his nose along my brow. "I know Christmas is a special time for you..."

When I thought he couldn't make me melt anymore, there he is, setting fire to my heart. I smile, stroking his hair. "I know this is a big one, so feel free to say no if you think it's too risky, but... could we join the masked Christmas Eve party? I've never been to anything like it, and the hotel is so beautifully decorated. I know for you Christmas time can be hard—"

He cups my face and silences me with a sweet kiss that still tastes of my cum. "Consider it done. I'll get us our costumes."

CHAPTER 18

CESAR

I'VE PROMISED ELI TO be the best boyfriend he could dream of, so of course I tracked down the man in a reindeer mask, whom I've seen him eye as we entered the hotel. The stranger was as lanky and tall as my precious jewel, and for the low sum of three thousand dollars, he was fine parting with his exquisite burgundy suit. The elegant outfit looks even better on Eli, though I've had to fold in the cuffs of his pants so they didn't appear too long. I do worry a little that his gray hair is visible, since that's a very recognizable part of the 'Festive Fugitive's' image, but he's combed the waves back into a short tidy ponytail, so I don't think it draws that much attention. Besides, with his face covered, people might just think he's way older.

My own attire was even easier to obtain. The hotel offers a rental service, so by the time my lamb and I leave our room, I'm a dark shadow stalking its flashy prey. The wolf mask I'm wearing with my black suit is oddly fitting.

"You look so handsome, Wolf," Eli grins at me, his gray eyes like two jewels.

Sure, attending a party has its risks, but he seems so happy I couldn't deny him anything.

We enter the huge event space lavishly decorated with real pine branches, colorful baubles, and chains of sparkling lights. Many of the guests are either dancing, laughing, or drinking at tables with snacks, all in their finery and masks. While a few people wear full costumes, like a sexy Mrs. Claus, or a Gingerbread Man, most men are in suits and masks like us, and most women in elegant evening gowns made of thousands of sequins, or tight velvet.

I've been to parties like this over the years, accompanying Sullivan, but never as a guest. And definitely not with a *boyfriend* on my arm. I'm so proud and giddy even the decor is growing on me. Maybe it's Christmas spirit filling my chest. Or the fact that I didn't come, and I'm horny, is conditioning me to like festive cheer. As if I have a hard-on for Christmas.

There are tables where guests can dine on food from an exclusive buffet, but I lead the way straight to the station with hot drinks, because if I'm ever to allow myself hot chocolate with cream, this is the night. On the stage, a classical singer starts a recital of winter-themed songs, but I only have eyes and ears for my lamb, who wants to see and experience *everything*.

Dancing together might draw too much attention, but if I could do it, I would, because he's not just another Friday. He is mine, and I want him to know it.

"Boozy hot chocolate? Don't mind if I do!" Eli laughs, adding a generous splash of rum to his drink. He's already tipsy, but I don't mind watching over him. It's his night. He can do whatever he wants. If he overdoes it, I'll carry him to our room and tuck him into bed.

He stalls, looking back at me and pointing to his glass. "Is this okay? Is it included in the price of the event?"

I can't take my eyes off him, and each twitch of his Adam's apple makes me thirsty for a taste of his skin, but this isn't the place, so I stroke his silvery hair and pull him close. "You can have whatever you want. The price is irrelevant, I just want you to enjoy yourself."

He takes a big sip, then grabs my hand. Before I realize what he's doing, he lifts it above his head and twirls under it. "Look at me. Reindeer Cinderella boy at the ball. I wish my family could know how much fun I'm having. Not Spencer. Spencer can rot in a ditch."

My gums itch, and I lean in to bury my face in his neck. The mask dulls his scent, but it's still there—fresh, and rich, and welcoming. I long to rub myself all over him, so I can carry those familiar notes on my own skin.

"I would kill him for you."

Our eyes meet in intense silence. He's considering it.

"No. He doesn't deserve your attention." Eli strokes my arm, and we might be making a bit of a spectacle, but fuck it. It's 2025. I will show my *boyfriend* affection if I damn well please.

The people here are polite enough to not stare, so I take that at face value. With two glasses of hot chocolate, we gravitate around the ballroom, listening to the heavenly soprano. But as beautiful as the singer's voice is, all I want to hear is my lamb's soft, happy laughter. Never before have I been with anyone like this. Occasionally, the men I fucked on Fridays would have dinner with me, or drinks at the very start of the night, but they were just distractions. Eli is the main event.

For once, I have someone to watch over and care for, but Eli wanting to return the favor makes all the difference. For once, I'm not a dog serving someone else's needs while waiting for a kick. I'm important, and allowed to want things.

It feels so damn good. I don't need alcohol, because I'm drunk on Eli's scent and taste. He's my indulgence, and I'm not even feeling guilty about this pleasure, because I'm free. Sullivan can't reach me, there is no implant in my heart, and for all I know, no one else knows the words that can bring me to my knees. Eli's burned them.

As I sit beside Eli on a plush couch, drinking my chocolate and listening to how he hopes for more cheery music later, I spot two people glancing at us from the corner. It's impossible for them to have recognized Eli. The little limp he has, happened already after his escape from the crime scene, so that can't be a tell. The other reason they might be looking makes the hairs on my body bristle and my breath hitch.

The problem with having a boyfriend others can see is that they might ogle him. They daren't approach when I'm around, surely? But what if we part? It's not unreasonable for Eli to want to use the restroom at some point. What if one of those onlookers decides to flirt with him there?

My lamb might be self-conscious about his body, but he cuts such a striking figure in the burgundy suit, long-legged like the animal he's dressed as, and I know for a fact that those two men aren't the first ones who've stared.

I slide my hand into his and squeeze it, wishing to anchor him with me. "Happy?" I ask, eager to have all his attention. Right now I'm feeling sorry I hadn't made him stay with me in our room and made love to him all night, but that would have been selfish. I want him to have everything, not just the things I find convenient.

Eli has eyes only for me when he sets down his glass and strokes the side of my mask. "Cesar... I thought my life ended when I shot Sullivan. But now I see it's only begun. I'm so happy here with you. And this party? You're making my dreams come true." Our masks bump into each other when he leans in, but it doesn't stop him from leaving a gentle kiss on my lips.

I've been with *countless* men. I've tried out unusual practices, and experimented with my own boundaries, but the soft, gentle touch of his lips holds way more power over me than even the kinkiest sex. My toes curl, and I slide my arm around him, itching to have him close. To never let go. To always fall asleep wrapped in a veil of his scent.

"So you'll stay with me?" *Even if my heart is too tainted to love?*

Eli snorts. "What's that question even mean at this point?"

But I don't get to answer. The two men who earlier watched us approach our couch and they both smile.

"Hey, I'm Carl." The man extends his hand to me, so I shake it, but my heart almost jumps out of my chest when he squeezes Eli's hand next.

I know it's absurd. Irrational. Borderline insane. But anyone touching Eli, even in this way, makes me want to snarl and bite.

"And I'm Timoly," says the other guy, making me pause. What kind of name is that? "We spotted you guys across the room, and wondered if you want to check out the private party. I can assure you it's *much* more interesting."

This isn't my first rodeo. "Are you inviting us to an orgy?"

Carl blinks behind his mask, but he doesn't lose his composure and smiles. "Participation is optional. We have two rooms, and one is meant for drinks and conversation."

"Gentlemen only," Timoly adds, eyeing me with unrestrained hunger. Did they not invite enough tops, or something?

"We're not inter—" I start saying, but then glance at Eli whose eyes are wide as saucers. "Or are we...?" The last thing I want to do is disappoint him when his life has been so hard. This is supposed to be *his* night.

I'm not letting anyone touch him, but we're adults, we like fucking. Watching an orgy isn't that different from watching porn.

Eli licks his lips. "Participation is *optional*? What about clothes? Would we have to be naked?" Pragmatic about these matters as usual. I smile, thinking about that first breakfast together, when he casually discussed what kind of sex he likes over eggs.

"Don't you worry, no one's going to tear your clothes off. Unless you want them to," Timoly says, and I swipe my thumb across my man's palm, though I'm unsure whether I want to reassure *him* or myself.

"What do you think?" I ask, even though what I want is to take him upstairs and fuck him until his hole makes that hot squelching noise that always gets me.

He bites his lip with a naughty smile, and I already know what he wants. "Should we...? I kinda wanna see."

Carl seems a bit more reserved than Timoly whose horny pheromones I can almost smell through his jacket. "We also have our own bar down there and a chill area where you don't have to worry about the straights causing a scene," he adds.

Eli sits up straighter and nods at me excitedly.

That's settled then.

I rise, making sure my hand never leaves Eli's skin. "Lead the way."

I half expect the party to be in one of the large apartments, but the two men lead us downstairs, where hallways have lower ceilings, and the carpets—a rich red shade. Whoever's organizing this secret event, they must be doing it with the silent acknowledgement of the management. Otherwise, Carl and Timoly wouldn't have led us into an 'Entertainment Area' within the hotel.

"It feels like going to a speakeasy during the Prohibition," Eli whispers and bumps his small antlers against my stiff wolf ears.

I have to admit his enthusiasm is rubbing off on me. But it's when he squeezes the top of my thigh that I start to wonder whether the orgy offers private rooms where we could let off some steam. Do I regret not getting off with him when he offered earlier? Maybe a little, but it will make fucking him later all the sweeter.

"Welcome to our kingdom," Carl announces as he opens a door at the end of the underground corridor with no windows.

I half expect that this is an ambush by some of Sullivan's stragglers and stiffen, ready to maim and kill, but no, we are led through a thick velvet curtain to a room resonating with a mix of slow, sensual electronic music and moans. I'm hit with a dense cloud of diffused perfume, liquor, and distilled lust. The lights are dimmed, the whole space has a warm coloring of reds, a few pink spotlights, and black walls that cool off the boudoir vibe. While a few Christmas decorations feature here in the form of tinsel and pine, there are no baubles. After all, no one wants to risk breaking one and then sitting their naked ass on it.

Just as Carl and Timoly said, clothing is optional. Some men, like us, are fully dressed, while others don't even have a single sequin to cover their nakedness. I have my arm around Eli's waist as he looks around wide-eyed. Closer to the door, men seated on black leather couches talk, drink, and watch a stripper in a jockstrap resembling a Santa hat dance around a pole. But my hearing is just as sharp as my sense of smell. Farther down, behind wide open doors, there's skin slapping against skin, moans loud enough to be heard over the music, and I spot a naked man passing from that room to this one. He is wearing a half-mask that transforms him into a rabbit-human hybrid with a huge erection jutting from above a leather cock ring.

Carl waves his hand toward the couches and the other room. "If you're feeling lost or need anything, just approach the bartender. Other than that, have fun!" Did he wink at Eli? He better not have.

"Merry Christmas," I mumble into Eli's ear as strangers assess the new arrivals. It's not too crowded. I can see, perhaps ten guys, though I assume there's more of them where the horny rabbit came from.

"Oh my, God," Eli whispers and squeezes my hand. "Is it okay to look? I've never been to something like this."

"We can later go farther in. How about a drink first?" I ask, leading him to the bar manned by a bartender dressed in the same outfit I've seen on all other staff members. I order a mocktail for myself, and a piña colada for Eli, then lean against the counter to take in the atmosphere.

A man wearing a green velvet suit eyes us with something more than curiosity, but I choose to ignore him and focus on my lover, who stares at the stripper showing off his considerable skills. "You can look, but don't touch,"

I tell him, whispering straight into his silver hair. Later tonight, I'll pull the band off his hair and make it messy again, the way I like to see him after a long fuck.

Eli holds up his hand. "Oh, I wouldn't! I'm just curious about it all. You're still the most handsome guy here anyway." He grins and gives me a kiss. "But you... You won't miss this, right? Picking a different guy each Friday?"

How is that even a question when I feel so safe in his presence I've dozed off with my head in his lap? But he is serious, so I clear my throat and bring his hand to my lips. "I wasn't *picking* them. I was binging on enough sex to tide me over to the next week. They really were just bodies, because I wasn't allowed any attachments," I say as my gaze drifts toward two laughing guys on the other end of the bar. One of them wears only a candy-cane patterned jockstrap, the other—a tight Santa outfit, complete with a fake beard.

"No, I'm not *Santa!*" he exclaims to his friend. "Don't you see the wavy wig?" He points to his head and picks up the hat to show off his silver hair. "I'm the Festive Fugitive."

The other man rolls his eyes. "Hm. Bit grim."

"Is it? The guy took out some serial killer-level psycho. Good riddance, if you ask me. Literally gay twink icon. Hope they never find him. What do you guys think?" He pulls down his beard to have a sip of his margarita and looks at us. "Festive Fugitive. Yay or nay?"

Eli smirks. "What do you think, Wolf? Yay or nay?"

A warm shiver descends my back when he calls me that, but I don't let anyone see how much of an effect this has on me and shrug. "Law is corrupt. That is why we should all be pro-justice rather than pro-law. If I ever get the chance to meet the Festive Fugitive, I'm going to give him the head of his life."

The two men down the bar laugh and raise their glasses while Eli hides his big smile behind his piña colada. He's so adorable I want to take him to the back rooms already. Me as the wolf, him as my prey.

"He might be the only guy I'd let my boyfriend fuck who isn't me." Eli winks at me and pulls on my hand. Seems he's ready to explore.

"Isn't he right here, though?" the Santa asks, spreading his arms to show off the way the red coat opens to reveal a smooth chest.

"I'm sure there will be takers," I tell him, making it playful so his ego remains unbruised as I let Eli pull me toward the doorway dividing us from a room that smells of sweat, cum, and poppers.

"I think it would stress me out to be here on my own," Eli whispers as his gaze drifts off to ogle a couple going at it on a couch under red lights.

"Why?"

"I don't know. I guess I'm more of a boyfriend type. I don't want some stranger's hands on me, no matter how hot he might be."

"Good," I say and sip on my mocktail as the other room reveals itself in its dusky glory.

"For the other guy," Eli teases with a smirk. He knows me too well.

It's not that big of a party, but there are more than enough guys within sight to satisfy everyone. The furniture is clad in easily removable covers some poor soul will need to launder first thing tomorrow, but it's Christmas Eve, and quite a few of the men I'm seeing are intent on collecting their presents early.

The colorful spotlights pulse to the rhythm of the music, as if this whole interior, and all the bodies within it are sharing the same pulse.

"He better keep his hands to himself," I say, watching a broad-shouldered guy fuck someone in the very back. Three weeks ago, this could have been me, desperate to satisfy all my cravings on a single Friday evening.

Now I'm not beholden to any masters, yet here I am, craving the same man every single day.

As we drift to a wall offering an excellent view of the entire space, I sense Eli's pulse quickening when I move my thumb over his wrist.

"I bet you now regret you didn't get off," he teases and slides his hand over my cock.

Bad boy.

"That's... so cruel," I whisper, retracting my hips until my ass is flat against the wall. But hope rises inside me. He can't remove his mask, or reveal any identifying marks, but he *could* jerk me off...

Would that be enough to let off some steam at this point? I do like that even with all the studs and fucking around, his attention is still on me.

Eli downs his drink and grins. "I don't know how I'd feel about someone watching us fuck. I think I'm too shy for that after all. Even in the mask. I want only you to see my body open up and my legs tremble."

Oh, he is *so* doing this on purpose. Planting the idea in my head so a mix of jealousy and arousal twists me up. I'd say he will regret it later, but he'll probably enjoy the hell of the rough fuck I'll unleash on him.

"You're teasing me," I say, pulling him back to the bar space. "Is that what good boys do to their boyfriends?"

"Who said I'm a good boy?" Eli asks, picking up my hand and licking the sensitive part between my thumb and forefinger. The shiver it elicits goes all the way to my dick. He's drunk. But I like seeing him like this. Free and playful.

He's quite possibly the handsomest man I've ever laid eyes on. How can I resist him?

"You two probably can't wait to join the fun in the other room," Timoly says, appearing at our side out of nowhere, his eyes flickering behind the simple mask he's wearing. I swear that name has to be fake.

I chuckle and lean in to kiss Eli. "Hardly. I don't think this is our scene."

The man who invited us here seems to have had an agenda from the start, because he barely keeps back a scowl. "Understandable. I also prefer a more... intimate setting, if you catch my drift."

He wants a threesome.

Or a foursome with Carl, or whatever the other man's name was, in the peace of their apartment.

"Sure you can't talk your wolf into a bit of an adventure?" Timoly asks, stepping closer to Eli, and setting my senses on high alert. He thinks Eli is the weak link and can be swayed. Or that I'm under Eli's heel, which isn't untrue. Both options piss me off though.

Eli shakes his head. "Yeah, I don't think *my wolf* wants a different guy."

I like that he now has the confidence to know that.

To my astonishment, Timoly doesn't get the hint. He slides his hand around Eli's waist and looks me straight in the eye as if it's some sexy game we're playing when he's about to lose his damn life. "You wanna watch *me* fuck your boy?" Timoly asks, voice thick with lust.

I don't even get to think before my hand is tight around his wrist, twisting the bastard's arm. He's releasing a trail of hisses, but I only let go once his dirty hands are no longer on my lamb.

I growl, showing him all my teeth. Fury is like a drug soaking my brain, but I'm still reining it in, still in control until that fucker opens his stupid mouth again.

"Jesus fucking Christ, man! It's not like his sloppy hole is such a prize!"

My blood is on fire, but Timoly is ready for my fist and leans to the side, escaping the punch meant to make him bleed. Not for long. I step forward, caging him to the wall, and when the stink of fear teases my senses, I sink my teeth into his cheek and bite until the flesh gives.

He screams out and pushes on my shoulders in desperate panic, but I don't let go. Play with fire, prepare to get burned. He tries to kick me in the balls, but I expect it and kick his feet from under him. Timoly might have the guts, but he's no fighter. We go down, but I don't let go of his cheek until I taste blood.

The screaming intensifies. He pounds on my chest, but when he tries to punch my head, I grab his wrist. This is the fucking hand he slid to my Eli's waist. When he wiggles it around instead of accepting his punishment, I shift my fingers to the right spot and snap the bone in his wrist.

I didn't want to cause a scene. I really didn't. But then he asked for it with his goddamn shit-spilling mouth. His blood on my tongue only fuels my anger.

He thought he'd be fucking *my boyfriend*?

The only thing that's getting fucked is the hole I'm making in his cheek.

"Wolf! No!" Eli yells, and I realize this is the third time he's saying that as he pulls on my shoulder.

"Call the cops!" the bartender screeches somewhere in the background.

Carl and a stranger that might as well be made of air are ready to stop me when I get up, but when I stare them down from behind my mask, with Timoly's blood dribbling down my chin, both of them lose their courage. My gaze drifts to Eli's face, and the shock painted over it makes the dog inside me cower in shame. I've made a mess of things, and now he'll have to pay the price.

"Let's go," I mumble, placing my hand on his shoulder and pushing him forward.

Timoly's crying, Carl is once more considering a step forward, but the growl I make at him comes from somewhere deep within my chest. It's primal, protective, and territorial.

He steps aside, and Eli runs as fast as his limp allows, knowing I am right behind him.

Fuck.

At least his mask is still on.

CHAPTER 19

ELI

We're on the run from the cops, and maybe I should worry my actions from three weeks ago might catch up with me because of a jealous fit, but I'm warm, inside a car smelling of real pine, and there's alcohol in my veins, so I can't help but find this whole situation hilarious.

I laugh, again remembering Timoly's face the moment Cesar bit into him as if he were a piece of jerky. I probably shouldn't find my man mauling another person funny, but I'm drunk, okay? For once in my life I have someone who'll stand up for me, so no, I don't find his fury or jealousy off-putting. In fact, the blood smeared around his mouth turns me on. He hasn't even removed his mask, so he's still a very elegant, if feral, wolf.

"It'll be fine, you'll see," Cesar says from the driver's seat as he takes another fast turn along a narrow road he found in the huge book of maps the previous owner of the SUV kept in the glove compartment. "I don't even hear any sirens. It's kinda freeing, you know? There's a manhunt for me because of the murder, so how much worse can it get really?"

He glances my way, then switches the headlights to full beam, revealing more of the snow-covered forest. "I'm sorry. I should have kept my cool."

"It was a bit much, but fuck it, he deserved it. Maybe he'll learn from this. And it's not like I wanted to stay at the orgy anyway." I shrug and stroke Cesar's thigh with a grin. He's all the man I need. Though that penthouse suite would have been a nice place to wake up in on Christmas Day. But I don't need him to feel any more guilty.

His muscles twitch at my touch, and once again he peeks my way, jaws set as if he were in a continuous fight with his own temper. I no longer fear him though. "Damn right, he deserved it! Who does that fuck think he is?"

I can't help but giggle. "The orgy king I guess. *Timoly*. Fake-ass fucking name. He's either married, a pastor, or the CEO of Family United. Wonder how he'll explain the injury to either his wife, congregation, or board of investors. 'Oh, I was out doing charity work, and out of nowhere, this feral child attacked me!'"

A choked sound that resembles a laugh leaves Cesar's mouth as he stares at me wide-eyed. The dried blood around his lips transforms the expression into the satisfied smile of a sated beast, and I find myself wanting to kiss him.

"You're so fucking hot right now," Cesar mumbles.

"Me? Is it my antlers?" I smirk and pull the mask back down over my face.

The car slows down quite abruptly, and the safety belt digs into my flesh as Cesar changes course and finally stops between two large trees. I'm watching him when he frees himself from the seatbelt, only to reach across my body.

The back of my seat sinks under my weight until it's completely flat.

I gasp as I drop, and my excitement spikes in an instant, because I'm pretty sure I know what he wants. I can't open my seatbelt fast enough. I glance back at Cesar as he climbs over the gearbox. With the moonlit sky as his background, his dark silhouette looks otherworldly. The tall ears of the wolf mask amplify what a beautiful predator he is. I'm more than happy to be his prey.

"I would not exchange you for any other man at that orgy," Cesar rasps, bracing himself over me, his knee pressing on the seat between my spread legs. "You are one in a million."

I'm already reaching for his belt, eager to sate all his desires. "Maybe you do love me then?" I tease in the darkness. I know he's been through unimaginable cruelty, but I see that spark in him, even if he doesn't.

Cesar stills over me, his eyes in deep shadow as I listen to his hurried, shallow breath. I can smell blood on him, but also musky perfume, and soap. It's a concoction so addictive I lean in to kiss him before silence forces him to answer.

He sinks into my lips as if they were his lifeline, hands dragging down my pants and underwear with a force a single man should not have. And yet, here he is. My beast.

The seat is warm under me, and the tightness of the space in the car makes me feel as though we're in a dark cocoon from which I never want to emerge. I gasp in satisfaction when I pull Cesar's cock out of his pants, and it's already hard for me.

My heart beats faster, and my body awakens as we fumble a little to get my pants off halfway. I just need one damn shoe off to give him all the access he wants. It's hard to focus when all I want is to slide the fingers of my other hand under his bloodied shirt, but I wedge the heel of my shoe against the glove box and manage to slide it off. From there, he grabs my thighs and lifts them with a growl that fits his wolf mask.

Oh how I want to be devoured. My ass clenches in excitement and my balls tighten when he drags the garment off me and then pushes my legs wide apart. There's such power in his body—a power that ought to be intimidating, yet all I feel is safety. My wolf has chosen me, and he will stand between me and danger for as long as he breathes.

A dark shiver makes my whole body arch when he loudly inhales the scent of my face, only to dig in. The sensation of teeth closing on my cheek has me jerking with confusion. Is it fear? Pleasure? Both? I don't care anymore. All I know is that I long for him to *consume me* and never let go.

"All mine," Cesar growls, pulling on my flesh, but just as the discomfort is about to become too much, his jaws open, and the soothing tongue glides over my pulsing skin.

I breathe hard when our eyes meet for a second and lust sparks between us like lightning. "All yours..."

His fingers slide over my naked thigh, and to my ass where he grabs me hard. His nails dig into my flesh as his lips descend to my jaw where he teases me with another bite. And another.

The groan he makes has me rubbing my stiff cock against him, but he's not done yet, and when I attempt to close my legs around him, he grabs both sides of my fancy shirt to rip it open. Buttons fly off, but all I care about is the way he's watching me as he descends on my flesh, biting into my pec as if he really plans to feed on me.

"Oh, I wish I could hide inside your skin," Cesar rasps.

"You can," I whisper, stroking his thick cock. It pulses with need in my hand. "I want you inside me." I've never been in such an emotional frenzy when fucking. He satisfies all my needs and there is no loneliness when Cesar is with me. He fills every dark corner within me with the fire burning deep inside him.

"Yes," he responds in a whimper and fucks my hand with that pulsing cock as he sucks on my nipple. We're on the side of the road, and anyone passing by could see us, but I don't care. All I want is to let him crawl inside and fill me with heat.

He plucks lube out of his pocket and drops it on my chest, still making those impatient movements with his hips. "I need it now. Need you."

I'm quick to get some lube in my hand and on his cock. I look between us, overheating already. My legs are spread for him, and his dick is so rigid. It even twitches, as if Cesar is that excited to be inside me. I'd lube my ass for him too if it wasn't too awkward in this position.

"Go on, fill me. You're so hot like this. My gorgeous monster." I bite my lip in excitement, already antici-pating the rough ride.

I love it when he loses his composure during sex, so desperate all he can do is use me until his balls are empty. It's the hottest thing I've ever experienced, and I can't get enough of it.

"Oh f-fuck..." he mutters, folding me so fast I end up pressing my feet to the roof of the car. That's how he's going to have me—in this uncomfortably tight, awkward space, because I've given him permission to help himself to my body whenever he needs it, and he is too aroused to wait.

I'm in fucking heaven.

We both gasp when his hard dick presses at my entrance, and the faint moonlight captures his face just right, allowing me to see his intense gaze, and the blood smeared on his face. Blood he spilled *for me*.

"You're always so tight," he whispers, making my cheeks heat up.

"Or is your dick just that thick?" I tease and give his lips a lick, but then moan as soon as his slippery cockhead slides over my hole. I'm so sensitive there my toes curl.

"You know how to compliment a man properly," Cesar whispers with a dark chuckle, but then he's braced over me, and enters.

Each inch he pushes in makes me more breathless. By the time he's all the way inside, I'm shivering under him and can't stop it if I tried.

No man has ever felt this good.

My chest tightens at the sudden realization that it will never be enough. I will always crave him.

"Oh, I will make you overflow so very soon," Cesar whispers, licking my ear.

I whimper, grabbing his shoulders. The fabric of his suit is so silky, its elegance in such stark contrast with the killer underneath. "Yes. Please. I love it when you come inside. Love feeling your dick pulsing in me." My own cock is already dribbling pre-cum onto my stomach, because being fucked by Cesar is such a turn-on I can come on command when he stretches my hole.

I choke on a moan when he retracts his hips, only to stab into me, gaze never leaving my eyes, as if he wants to feast on my reactions.

"My sweet lamb, you're stuck with me now. I am never letting you leave my side," he rasps, and when I reach for him, he grabs my wrists and holds them down above my head.

The gesture makes my cock twitch in excitement. Yes. I'm at his mercy now. I'm his puppet to do with as he pleases. A warm hole he can take pleasure in. I gasp when he descends on my neck with teeth and kisses while his hips start moving, first at a languid pace, then faster.

My legs are open to him, my chest exposed, neck offered if he wants to feast on me. I truly feel what it means to be his.

"Fuck... Fuck... yes. Just like that," I beg helplessly as he rides my hole in any way he likes. At first, he teases me by keeping the thrusts shallow, fucking me at an angle that doesn't quite let him hit the spot I need stimulated. Once he's intent on making me come, pleasure goes into overdrive as he assaults my prostate over and over. I tense, pressing both feet against the roof.

The wolf mask is still on, and I force my eyes open, imagining he's a real beast going to town on its mate. Claiming him. Breeding him.

He stops. Then goes shallow again, as if to show me he's in charge.

"You're so hot inside," Cesar groans against my skin, gripping my wrists even harder. "Go on, squeeze me, milk my dick."

I'm so brainless I don't question it, just clench my muscles, time and time again for his pleasure. His moans are my prize. Happy, guttural, horny. I swear I can smell his arousal among the intense scent of pine in the car.

"*Such* an obedient hole."

The dirty praise makes me whimper and squirm, because I want to come so bad, and he knows it.

"Deeper. Please, fuck me deeper."

He knows exactly what I mean.

"Here?" His grin when he stabs into me is halfway demonic with that mask and blood smeared around his lips.

"Yes!" I cry out, unable to stand the pressure. "I need to come."

Finally, the beast stops toying with his food. He lowers his whole weight on me, and while claiming my neck with his mouth, fucks me into oblivion.

I come so hard I can't tell if I'm seeing stars under my eyelids, or if the roof of the car has opened up. It must be the former, because my feet still scrape against the headlining fabric. I clench and unclench my fingers, helpless under Cesar, and oh so happy about it.

He plows me with abandon, though I'm barely lucid by the time he finishes, flooding my insides with his cream.

I'm floating in the heat of his arms, and when my eyes are closed, it's so easy to pretend we're out in the open, spreading a blanket deep in the woods, and he's going to soon drag me to his lair.

But as appetites are satisfied, the merciless beast is gone, replaced by a sweet pup who showers my face with kisses.

I don't know how much time passed for me to get down from my high but I look at him with a smile, all sweaty and sated. Cesar's mask is off, and mine must have fallen off at one point or another, so it's just us.

"Oh! Wait. I've got something." I suddenly remember and reach into the pocket of my jacket. It's a bit crumpled, but I grab the mistletoe I swiped from the hotel lobby, and lift it over my head with an expectant smile.

Cesar's gaze follows it, but then he shakes his head. "You're a very good reason to enjoy Christmas," he says before pressing his lips to mine.

Who would have thought murder could bring such happiness? I certainly didn't. Even as I fantasized about killing Sullivan, I never had a clear escape route or any idea about what a life *after* would entail. I couldn't see a future for me. At best, I thought I'd run away and forever live off grid out of my car. Or... something. Now, Cesar and I, we have a goal.

"No more fancy hotels though. It was amazing while it lasted, but too risky. We really need to go." I stroke Cesar's head and throw the mistletoe to the backseat.

He sighs and kisses my hand. "I know. It's just that... I wanted to make this Christmas special for you."

"You already did, Cesar. *You* are the best, most surprising gift I couldn't have imagined getting." I have so much tenderness for him my heart aches and overflows with it.

Cesar rests his head on my chest and kisses my still-flushed skin, then glances at his wristwatch when it pings. "Ha. It's already the twenty-fifth."

My heart skips a beat in excitement. "Merry Christmas!" Maybe a bit weird to say that when we're half naked and his cum is oozing out of me, but I don't care.

His smile is joyful when he kisses me again. "Merry Christmas. Soon, we will be far away from here, and you won't have to run ever again."

"So... what's it like? The place we're going?" I was too wrapped up in our travel and escape that I didn't even give it much thought. I just trusted him. And I still do.

Cesar strokes the back of my head, watching me as if he couldn't imagine there being anything more important than this moment. "I have the house in Alaska on this small island. Very private. I suppose that will be my Christmas gift, but I figured... you might still enjoy a little token so..." He stretches, reaching into the glove compartment, and returns to me with a little box.

My eyes widen and it's as if the sound of jingling bells resonate through my body with glee. "You got me something? And we're doing gifts early? Yes, yes, let's do that," I babble in excitement.

He clears his throat, shy like he hadn't sawed into me as if he'd been deprived of sex for years. "Don't get too excited. It's just this little thing I picked up during a stop."

He presents me with a small box and I open it to a simple charm bracelet. An enameled Christmas tree with two rhinestones hangs off it next to a silver heart. It's insanely cute, and while I've never worn anything like it, I already know that once it's around my wrist, I will never take it off.

"I know this is meant for girls, but I wanted you to have something that references how we met. And you love Christmas, so I thought... you might enjoy this, at least sometimes," Cesar says, staring down at the box. "I wasn't really in a position to get you something better while we traveled, but if you hate it, you can pick something else."

I snort and stroke his face, holding out my other hand so he can put it on for me. "Dumbass. I love it."

His eyes dart up to meet mine. "That... yeah, that makes me happy," he says and fastens the bracelet around my wrist. It's cool to the touch, but not for long, because when he presses his face to my hand, all I can feel is warmth.

"I've got a little something for you too. Wait." I twist out of his grasp so I can reach my backpack.

"Is this it?" Cesar asks and gives my ass a little slap.

"No! Just wait."

I finally get back to him with the little parcel, no bigger than my hand, wrapped in one of the newspapers we had at the cabin.

"I wasn't exactly able to buy anything, so I made you a little something."

Cesar accepts my gift with open hands and, after confirming it's okay to unwrap it already, peels back the packaging. I worked on it when he was out doing things around the house. It's a papier mâché bauble I painted red, attached a string for hanging, and decorated with some stars in Sharpie. In an oval I cut out of paper I painted in our initials and the year.

I swallow as I stare at it, realizing it not only doesn't look like much, but is also extremely cheesy. "It was something my parents did before my mom died. They made a bauble for every year together and hung it on the Christmas tree."

Cesar turns my gift in his hands. It's so very quiet I can hear the increasingly frantic beating of my own heart. I'm about to fill the silence when my man opens his mouth and speaks in a dull, strained voice. "I'm sorry you lost them."

"I couldn't help my mom. At least I got to avenge my dad. We didn't always see eye to eye, but I wish I could have done more for him. In the end, there's no changing the past." But I do see a future when I see the bauble in Cesar's hands. One in which we hang this ugly thing on our tree, in *our* house.

"This is…" He inhales, shaking his head as his gaze swipes up my face. "The best gift I've ever gotten. You're so talented."

I know him well enough by now to see that he's not saying everything he wants to but I don't want to press when the mood is so nice. He must just be thinking about all those shitty Christmases in Sullivan's service. "Hardly, but my crafting materials were limited." I give him one more kiss. "Do we want to start driving or get some sleep here?"

He pulls me close, burying his nose in my hair. "Let's go. We should take the first ship sailing to Alaska."

The tiniest knot twists in my stomach. I'm no mind reader, but something is off.

CHAPTER 20

CESAR

I's the best Christmas Day of my entire life. I shouldn't
be feeling so distraught, yet here I am, chewing on the
inside of my cheek as I wait for our food. The restaurant
is busy with people who, like me, don't crave a traditional
gathering with glazed ham as the main dish, but I try to
focus on something unrelated to the fact that the skin in
the middle of my chest is borderline itchy for no good
reason. I know for a fact I did not get any rash either,
because Eli and I have recently showered at a truck stop,
which means it's all in my head, just because of the tattoo
I ought to have before I board the ship.

I know why I'm increasingly obsessive about it, of
course, but I'm not crazy and know nothing's gonna happen if I retire without that final tattoo picked by Sullivan.

The fountain cascading through an artificial landscape
somewhere in a fantasy version of ancient China keeps

whispering to me, and I try to focus on its melody rather than on the clatter of dishes, the loud conversations—

"Sir, your food," the waiter says, presenting me with the paper bag smelling of General Tso's chicken, pepper steak, and fried wontons.

I thank him, leave a tip, and exit the restaurant, stepping out into the cold. It's just past midday, and as I cross the street, heading for the spot where we parked, I take note of the distant drum of festive music. I've gotten us a place on a ship heading for Anchorage first thing in the morning, but we still have to wait almost twenty hours until boarding, and the quiet area around the city park seemed like the safest bet to stay away from cameras that might capture Eli's face during the brief times he removes the fabric mask.

I told him to stay in the car and keep the doors locked, but I'm still relieved to see our vehicle where I left it, Eli intact, bobbing his head to the radio.

As soon as I open the door though and pass him the bag of food, I'm hit by the joyful Christmas tunes, because of course that's what he's listening to, and my stomach shrinks. I'm instantly reminded of what I shouldn't be thinking of and it's like a frustrating loop in my head.

I never finished my last job. I never got my last tattoo, the proof that I am free to walk away. But Sullivan's dead, so it shouldn't matter.

"Are you okay?" Eli cocks his head at me, pulling me out of the stupor.

Fuck. The last thing I need him worrying about is my fucked-up head.

"Yes, just a bit tired," I say, sliding into my seat and locking the doors. "Got you one of those bubble teas too. Hope you will enjoy *my* Christmas tradition."

"Chinese food? Sounds great. I'm just happy to be here with you." Eli's smile is so joyful when he looks my way. "I told you I could do some of the driving. We're in this together."

"I'd rather you can duck and hide at any moment. We're still not out of the woods," I tell him, stalling when my brain reminds me that without Sullivan's final gesture I might *never* feel truly out.

I know those are not logical thoughts, that a dead man can't have any power over me anymore. Nothing is stopping me from dropping everything and living however the hell I want, but I can't help feeling that the anchor that bastard had in me is still there, rusting inside my body, and poisoning every thought.

Even thinking about stepping on that ship makes me recoil. As if it's illegal. Not allowed. As though my brain refuses to accept that I can in fact go. The invisible cattle prod is there to shock me, and I'm losing appetite by the second.

"I don't know. I have a good feeling about it." Eli shrugs and starts shoveling food into his mouth, oblivious to my torment. I want it to stay that way. He has enough to deal with.

"A good feeling about—" I let it hang in the air, wondering if I've turned to my thoughts for long enough to miss a chunk of our conversation.

Again, I slide my hand under my top and scratch the itchy emptiness in the middle of my torso.

It's fine.

Sullivan is gone.

I don't need his permission to retire.

And yet, being this close to the port and planning an escape is making my skull feel too tight, and my chest—constrained.

Eli grins wider when he opens another paper bag. "Oooh! Fried wontons. Have I mentioned I love you?" He winks at me, but I don't have time to answer. "Look, they're preparing for a parade in the park. Any one of those Santas could be the Festive Fugitive." Eli wiggles his eyebrows and points farther in front of us, where a platform decorated to resemble a snow-covered mountaintop is surrounded by people in costumes.

I grab onto the empty skin under my clothes and twist the flesh, trying to distract myself with the discomfort of it. Sullivan no longer matters. Eli eliminated him from the game, and if I'm to be loyal to anyone, it's he who deserves it. How else am I supposed to ensure his safety than to escort him someplace where he's less likely to be found?

"They're not the real thing."

Eli smirks. "What if *I'm* the imposter and the real Festive Fugitive is now far away?"

It's becoming hard for me to focus even on Eli's jokes, which I love so much. The reality of leaving for Alaska in under twenty-four hours is hitting me in ways I never anticipated. Maybe it is weird that I'm not eating, nor responding to him like I normally would, but I'm in dire need of grounding myself, so I press my back to the seat and stare past the windshield, at the crowd preparing to set off with the parade. A pair of arms rises above all the moving heads, holding up a toddler, and all my muscles go rigid, as if the car accelerated to the speed of sound, forcing me to resist the unexpected pressure. A man in a Santa costume takes the child, and suddenly all I can think of is my fucking origin story.

Given away to Sullivan, I was a commodity gathering images in ink as if my own skin were a loyalty card, and the goal of filling it up—the freedom Sullivan tried to deny me. And now that card has expired before I could ever collect my prize.

I'm left denying myself the freedom in Sullivan's stead, as if that mechanism really is inside my heart and might explode the moment I set off for my journey north.

Somewhere beyond the choking in my throat and the darkness under my closed eyelid, I hear the rustling of paper and Eli's voice which can no longer reach me, because I'm drowning deeper and deeper inside my inner void.

Maybe this is the actual self-destruction mechanism Sullivan installed in me?

I was worried about the wrong thing.

My own body and mind are the biggest threats.

A hand on my back makes gentle circles, and it takes a while, but I finally hear Eli.

"Cesar? What is it? How can I help? Just breathe, okay?" he says softly as I realize I'm bent forward against the wheel and wheezing.

I shake my head, squeezing the steering wheel more tightly as the darkness retreats, leaving me back in a reality where I need to struggle with my greatest enemy, myself.

"I—sorry," I mumble, focused only on getting enough oxygen to avoid blacking out. Everything smells of pine, just like it had when my parents brought me to Sullivan, but those aren't the same pine branches. Those are mine and Eli's, and they have nothing to do with that monster of a man.

"Don't be. It's okay. I just need to know what's going on. How can I help? Do you need some water?" Eli passes me his bottle, still stroking my back as if I'm a child in need of comfort, not a grown-ass man twice his size, who could overpower him with ease.

How dare I be so weak when I promised him safety? It's embarrassing. He deserves someone better. Someone who won't fall apart because of a problem even I realize is all in my head. "No, it's not okay," I whisper, forcing words out of my aching throat. "I'm a burden."

"What? Of course you're not. Where is this coming from? You saved me, protected me, drive me around, buy me food. You're so thoughtful and a damn good fuck, so I really need you to spit it out. I sensed something was wrong hours ago. Whatever it is, we will deal with it together."

The stern note in his voice grounds me, and I feel seen when he admits that he sensed that something about my behavior was off. I can't hide from him, and I love it.

We might have only met three weeks back, but he sees me like no one before him.

His touch is warm, soft, reassuring, and I find myself melting into it as the pine branches drying inside the car surround us with their fresh scent. "It's... it makes no sense. There's something wrong with my head—"

He pulls me in until my head rests on his shoulder, and kisses my hair so gently I can no longer resist.

Not that I ever want to deny him anything.

"I'm fucked-up. Sullivan's dead, so is Lyle, I am free to go wherever I wish, but now that we're about to do that, it feels like I... can't," I finish, meeting Eli's eyes as shame sinks its claws into me.

He draws breath, about to speak, and I shake my head, because I am aware how crazy that sounds. "I know. It makes no sense whatsoever. You proved there's nothing inside my chest. I'm free, but I don't feel like I am. He might be dead and rotting six feet under, but he still has his leash on me."

Eli's kisses are so soothing I'm able to breathe again. "So what's stopping you? You did say you were supposed to retire, right? You were allowed to."

"Not without the final tattoo," I snap, shaking my head and scratching my torso through my clothes as a ringing echoes in both of my ears. "I would be free once that space over my heart was filled, but it's not. It's empty, and he kept denying me for the past two years. He just wouldn't pick a tattoo for me. I—just want it to be over," I whisper and rest my forehead against the steering wheel.

Eli's silent for a moment, then kisses my shoulder. "Okay, so... If he used to be your boss and command you, and make that decision about the tattoo, and I'm the one who killed him, am I in charge now? How about I choose a tattoo for you? End the cycle."

I spin my head to face him, and for the first time since I returned to the car, breathing is not a challenge. How did I not think about it myself? "Yes. Yes, please, can you do that for me?"

Eli latches onto my hands just as strongly as I hold his. "Sure. Let's do that. Any rules to it? Or can I just choose something to perfectly compliment your beautiful body?" He gives me another kiss, and I see it now. I'm worthy. His eyes overflow with love for me. If a broken mirror can still produce a reflection, then maybe the devotion of a broken man can be good enough too? I might never be capable of having feelings as pure as his are. But they're there, as broken and distorted as my past has made them.

I swallow hard and bring his hands to the buttons of my shirt. "It's meant to... commemorate the best job of the year."

Eli smiles and strokes my wrists with his thumbs. "Best blowjob?" he teases, and the change of topic is so unexpected I choke out a laugh.

"Don't think that's what Sullivan had in mind, but if you think that was the height of my skills in the past year..."

"Just messing with you, sweetheart. Give me your phone. I know just the thing. You sit back and eat, and I'll find someone in the area who I can coax into tattooing today."

My man is the most incredible person I've ever known, and if he allows it, I will make sure he never wants for anything. I kiss him, but fatigue has its claws deep in my flesh, so I sit back and start eating, trusting someone to take care of *me* for once.

How incredible is that?

My appetite is back, so I enjoy my food while Eli sinks into his phone.

It must be at least half an hour later when he takes a deep breath, puts down the phone and looks at me. "Hm... I... I'm sorry, Cesar, but it's Christmas Day. I even tried offering some people I managed to track down sizable bonuses if they come to do the job *now*, but no one's biting. Would you come to the back seat with me? I've got something there—Just come, okay?"

I squeeze my knees as disappointment washes over me in an icy wave. I should have expected this, but after having hope dangled in front of me, this feels as if something was taken away from me. Something I was promised.

But it isn't Eli's fault that the world won't align with our whims, so I take a deep breath, like when Sullivan forced me to endure pain for the sake of knowing how to, and leave the car.

The cold air helps, but when I'm back inside our cozy home on wheels, I have to brace myself so I don't fall apart again. I don't know how to deal with this issue though, so half my mind is elsewhere when Eli sits next to me and opens my jacket.

I clear my throat and point to the parade preparations not far away from where we're parked. "Eli, there's kids here..."

He groans and rolls his eyes. "I'm not trying to have sex. Just let me try something, okay? Take off your sweater."

I already know I'd give him anything he wants, and soon enough I'm sitting in the back of the car shirtless, the skin in the middle of my chest red from my nervous scratching.

Eli soothes it with some gentle stroking. "How about I... I mean, I will give you the ink, Cesar," he whispers and pulls out a black Sharpie. "Fill all this empty space." He smiles at me shyly and puts his hand over my heart, which responds by trying to knock through my breastbone and touch his palm. My gaze seeks his, and just like that, the shards inside me melt in the warmth of his gaze. How could I doubt him, when he's promised to help me?

"Please," I tell him softly, because my voice is threatening to break under the weight of the emotion welling up inside.

Eli leans in for a quick kiss, and the intense smell of the pen when he takes off the cap couldn't have been more soothing. I could inhale it and get high on it.

"Looking back, I think your best job was at our cabin," Eli says and it's hard to tell what exactly he's drawing when I look upside down, but I'm pretty sure it's a house by the rectangular shape. The pen glides over my skin, leaving marks that cover what was a blank canvas. "So that is taking center stage... And we have four threats eliminated, all for me."

I have to bite my lip not to snort at the cartoonish skulls he's drawing around the house. His is a completely different style than the somber, realistic images covering the rest of my torso, but I like it, because it reminds me of him.

He's the best thing that's ever happened to me.

"I am quite proud of that one."

Our eyes meet, his filling with glee. "But the picture wouldn't be whole if I didn't add some of the decorations we had in our cabin. The holly leaves we cut out, or the paper chains you so meticulously glued together..." Eli draws those as a frame around the house and skulls, taking his time to fill the whole space for my last tattoo.

He has talent. How come he hasn't shared that fact with me yet? I hope he can draw me too, or us, something to hang on the wall of the home we will soon share.

My thoughts come to a jarring, unexpected end, and I take a deep breath, feeling as if I'm tumbling off a cliff, frantically clinging to my hopes for safety, because *that* is what they are. Hopes.

When I first followed him into the night, making sure nothing happened to him during the flight from the gala, my goals were simple—to make sure he didn't suffer any negative consequences of freeing me, and the rest of the fucking world, from that crooked reptile Sullivan. When did it become more than that?

When did I start assuming Eli would follow my lead and want to retire with me? It's not fair to just project that onto him, when he ought to choose his own destiny once we're both safe.

I feel so selfish when he smiles at me and finally pulls away. "Okay. Wait, I'll take a photo so you can see if it's acceptable."

But even as he shows me the picture, I struggle to look at the screen, because I want to see *him* instead. He thinks I'm his savior, but he's the one who's saved *me*. Again.

I pull him close and press my lips to his forehead while my heart gallops, trying to absorb the ink.

Everything inside me longs to be close to Eli, to fall asleep with my head in his lap and fiercely protect him from anyone who dares come too close, but I shouldn't be selfish.

He took off my chains, and making sure he knows he's free to leave is the least I can do.

CHAPTER 21

ELI

Getting on board is nerve-wracking. Cesar has bribed someone to turn a blind eye to our presence on the ship, so technically we are not even registered as passengers. By the time we step onto the deck under the watchful eye of the seaman who looks as if he could hunt down a whale with a harpoon on his own, I'm too frazzled with stress to be afraid.

The man's beard is a pure white shade, just like the snow we are leaving behind in the glow of the artificial lights. It's around four in the morning, and bitterly cold, but if this plan pans out, I might really have gotten away with murder.

While the ship is primarily transporting cargo, we're not the only passengers. I've already spotted a couple with Go-Pros documenting it as an "*adventure*", and they aren't alone. Due to there being a very limited amount of cabins, most of the passengers will be setting up tents or sleeping on yoga mats in lounge areas, but my man can afford paying the premium for privacy. Still, as we walk along the railing and watch the massive port that could have been its own city, I'm eager to enjoy the fresh air for as long as possible, because I doubt we'll be socializing much while onboard.

I've got my cloth mask on, which is nice, because it keeps my face warm in the chilly wind. Both Cesar and I lean over the railing to watch the land disappear from a secluded spot so no one bothers us. I was so happy to help him with the tattoo issue. It felt like a special moment between us, like I was the only one who could save him from the trauma inflicted by Sullivan's brainwashing.

But now he's silent and distant again. Which makes me babble out of nerves.

"Did you visit the house we're going to often? Did you furnish it yourself? Or is it a bare bones situation?"

Cesar, who's been watching the lights on the shore, glances my way and clears his throat. "I've been there once. I used to rent it out to people, so it's furnished, but... well, redecoration is always a possibility," he says and offers me a flat smile. "We're off."

"Are you excited to retire? Or afraid you won't know what to do with your time?" I try and poke his hand with a gloved finger. The wind is so intense it would be hard to talk if we didn't stand so close. He swallows, and every second of silence shifts me closer to the edge of panic, because what is happening right now? Is he worried that this whole thing was a mistake? That I am a wedge in his plans for a peaceful life on his own?

Have I been too much again?

He clears his throat and speaks. "It still doesn't feel real. I wanted this for so long, I was angry when Sullivan delayed it, but I think deep down I didn't believe it could happen."

A sudden gust of wind swipes up my forehead and snatches my hat. We both bend over the railing to grab it, but it's too late. It's gone in the waves in seconds. I groan, because now my hair flaps about everywhere. We'll probably soon go to our cabin, but I don't want to leave this conversation unfinished.

"But you're happy now, right? That we're going there? Or are you questioning the location itself?"

The gasp he makes has my feet fusing with the steel floor, so I steady myself, pinning my gaze to his mouth. The cold wind rustles his dark hair in every direction as he grabs both my hands and leans his back against the taffrail. The stormy water, and the city cease to exist, because all I can see is him.

"We need to talk."

My stomach clenches, and I wonder if I should be jumping into the waves myself under the pretense of finding my hat. Our bubble is about to burst, and I don't want it to. Can I blame tears forming over my eyes on the wind?

"What did I do?"

Cesar's mouth goes slack. "What?"

I clench my hands on the railing. I can hardly breathe, but I'll get through this. I'm resilient, even if impulsive. "What do you want to talk about? I'm guessing I did something to… frustrate you?"

He licks his lips and squeezes my hands with more force. The cranes passing behind him are like monsters that might snatch my happiness away at any moment, but for now he's still here, touching me. "No, of course not! You're… you're the most incredible person I know," he shouts when the wind blows at us from the side, straight into our ears.

Cesar rolls his eyes and pulls me away from the gunwale, into a small, roofed space which, judging by the amount of cigarette butts littering the floor and the metal ashtrays, is frequented by smokers. Only one of its walls is open, and it faces another structure on the top deck.

"So what is it that you'd like to talk about? Is there a secret husband stashed away in that house?" I laugh nervously, but at this point, I'm ready for anything.

I have gotten way too invested in a new relationship, like I always do, and here comes the inevitable bucket of cold water. Too bad this time the disappointment will hurt more than all the previous times combined.

Still, I am an adult. I can take it.

Cesar swallows and once again squeezes my hands. "I'm used to thinking mostly about myself, but I don't want this to be just about what I want. I don't want you to feel trapped just because I'm helping you."

"Trapped..." I repeat, confused, wondering if he's trying to let me down gently. It's all very confusing, because just last night he told me how amazing I am, how I'm *his*.

He moves his hands up my arms and settles them on my shoulders. "I will help you. I will make sure you're safe, but you don't owe me anything. You are free to leave me, if you wish. I would still always take care of you," he says, ever quieter, until his voice disappears in the roar of the ocean.

I watch him, I listen, I understand the words he's saying, but they make no sense.

"I *do* owe you everything. Why would I want to leave?"

One of my exes did the whole 'oh, *I'm not good enough for you*' spiel just because he actually wanted to break up, but it doesn't feel like this with Cesar. There's something more here, and I'll get to the bottom of it.

Cesar swallows, his dark eye so intense it's like there's a storm brewing inside him. "I never want you to feel obligated to me the way I was to Sullivan. I'd kill a hundred more men just to be with you, and the beastly part of me wishes to keep you in my basement, but I..." his voice breaks a little, "I don't ever want you to feel like I did. Like I couldn't get out. You need to know you're free to leave, and I would help you do that. I'd establish you in some country far away—"

Suddenly I understand everything he's trying to say. All the tension inside me dissolves, and I close the distance between us to hug him.

"You love me."

He freezes, both his real eye and the fake one open wide, as if I was a snake that might kill him with a single drop of its venom. "I love you."

I pull the mask under my chin to kiss him. "I told you it's inside you. You care for me more than for the need to own me. That's unselfish. That's love. And I love you so much, Cesar. I don't need to go anywhere without you. I'll gladly and freely follow you to the end of the world."

He exhales, releasing air as if it's been choking him. "You promise? You're staying because you want to?" he asks in a voice so heartbreakingly tender I know that if I rejected him now, the wound would never heal.

But I'd never do that. I am his, and he is mine.

I nod, my arms wrapped around him. "Yes. There's nothing I want more than to live at your side."

His grip tightens around me, until my feet leave the deck, and he is pressing us so close together, not a single hair could sneak in between us. "I want to make you happy. So you never regret this."

"I have many regrets, Cesar. You will never be one."

He gives me another kiss, this time more intense, and I can only hope we don't have any spies around, because I can't stop myself when his hot tongue caresses mine, his lips so soft and warm. I wouldn't need a coat right now, because the heat that courses through my veins thanks to his love is enough.

He loves me.

It takes a while for us to stop, but eventually Cesar pulls away with a soft smile. "Let's go find our cabin. We'll be on board for a while. More than enough time for you to think about how you want to decorate our new home."

Home.

I feel like crying again. Before meeting him, I lived out of my car for over a year. Before that, my living arrangements were on shaky legs for years. And now I'll not only have a home with the man I love, but also money to decorate it, make it our sanctuary.

He leads the way out of the shelter. The wind has gotten worse now that we've left the port, so he shields me and leads the way toward the nearest staircase. The man who watched us board is still there, now wearing a woolen hat and a bright yellow jacket. He's only missing a long pipe to look like an old-timey seaman.

He stares into my eyes, which is uncomfortable in itself, but the way he steps toward us, eyes pinned to mine unnerves me.

"You're the Festive Fugitive." It's more of a statement than a question.

Suddenly, I'm all too aware that I lost my damn hat and my gray hair flaps about in the wind like a flag. My mask is pulled down after all the kissing because I'm a dumbass, so I just stand there, petrified and unsure what to do. By now, he might have already alerted the police over the radio.

I remain frozen when Cesar steps in front of me, a bull about to charge. Or throw the man overboard. And I—don't stop him, so maybe I'm not as good of a person as I always believed myself to be.

The seaman watches him with bright eyes, unfazed, as if he'd fought off the Kraken and wouldn't be intimidated by the likes of Cesar. "What? You're the one who didn't notice he removed the mask. At this rate, the whole ship will know we have a celebrity on board," he adds with a raspy chuckle.

I pull up my mask despite it being too late now. I also pull up my hood, which gets instantly blown back. My heart beats so fast I'm on the verge of fainting, but the man doesn't... seem antagonistic?

"Your secret's safe with me, kid. Good riddance, if you ask me. Go on." He shakes his head and steps back to the railing to let us through. "And hide that mop on your head. You got this far, don't ruin it."

I swallow and nod, not bothering to smile, since the mask would now hide it. "Thank you. I will." I pull my hood on, and this time keep it in place with my hand.

If Cesar thanks him too, he does it in silence. My reality is overwhelming, so I walk on weak knees and let my man steer me in the right direction, just like he has since we met. For once, I don't have to carry all the burdens myself, I have someone to shoulder them with me.

Someone who loves me, and for whom I matter. Someone to cherish, and to spend every Christmas with. Someone for whom I'd kill or die.

"Alaska, here we come," I say as soon as we're in our cabin, and hug Cesar.

He closes me in his strong arms, and I know I'm safe already.

EPILOGUE

CESAR

One year later.

"A year on since Arthur Sullivan's violent death, we are still left with questions. We might never know what became of Elijah Ward, also known as the Festive Fugitive, after he fled the police. But the anniversary of the event that shook America is not without controversy. Ward's supporters have gathered for spontaneous rallies in many of our cities, protesting against corruption in politics, but many commentators point out that unlawful deaths should not be celeb—"

I switch off the TV, cutting the anchor off just before she can start a conversation with one of the so-called commentators, but both Eli and I have had enough of this whole Festive Fugitive business. For us, life has gone on, and we're planning to celebrate our second Christmas together.

Our massive tree takes up a whole corner of the living room and reaches all the way to the ceiling. We set it up at the start of December, as that was what Eli wanted, but we've been making decorations for it since summer, and I'm proud to say it's paid off. The theme is celebrating our life in Alaska, so we went with mostly blue and silver. We have handmade paper chains, painted baubles, cut-outs of seals and moose stuck to cardboard, and lots of wooden stars.

The decorations are also all over our house, and I loved hanging them all up with Eli. We're building the kind of home I've never had. The kind Eli lost and can get back now we're together.

As a trained killing machine I never thought I'd enjoy gluing together snowmen out of felt pom-poms, but it's exactly what I need to soothe my soul.

"How is it going?" I ask, placing the remote next to a wreath Eli weaved only a week ago. He is so talented when it comes to all things craft and DIY. He puts me to shame with both a glue gun and a drill, but since the big jobs often require two people, I'm happy to be ordered around.

"Almooost there..." he says, leaning over the table, and staring into a mirror. "Done!" The brown contact lens slots into place, hiding his natural bright gray.

"Just let me know if you need to remove it," I say, approaching him through the spacious living room.

It's modern, with clean lines and lots of wooden elements, but all the personal touches Eli added while recovering from plastic surgery are what truly give our place personality.

One of the walls is painted in a lattice of abstract patterns, and while I wasn't sure about that choice when I initially followed Eli's vision, I now appreciate how it livens up the vast space furnished with comfortable modern furniture. This is where we watch movies, where we read books, and sometimes even do crafts together. Where we fuck like bunnies when the upstairs bedroom feels too far away.

To the right is our open-plan kitchen, with a huge island that allows us to work together without arguing over one of us blocking the other's way. Additionally, the counter is at a very convenient height for our favorite non-cooking purposes, so... well, let's say I seize every opportunity to feel like it's Friday.

I never imagined I could be this happy here. Only now I see that. I expected peace. I thought that every now and then I might have someone over for sex, or that freedom would mean no orders from Sullivan, but before Eli, I never got to experience what that would be like.

With Eli, it's more than I could have imagined. Our life is not always peaceful, and that's the beauty of it. Sure, sometimes we get cozy on the couch, make some boring instant noodles, or watch birds from the porch, but Eli is so active it's usually not long between one burned pan apocalypse and a day-long rant about something going 'wrong' on the TV show we're watching.

I love that chaos, it makes me feel alive. Like I'm important to him. I can gut a fish for him so he doesn't gag over it, I'm in charge of our boat, I clean the living room when his paper crafts get out of hand, and I always make sure all the candles are put out before we go to bed.

I wouldn't have to do most of that if he wasn't here. But I love that I do. He's my perfect match, makes me laugh every day, fulfills my deepest desires, showers me with praise, and without him here, my life would be comfortable but... empty. Colorless. With no purpose.

I'm unsure whether I communicate it to him well enough, but he did save me in more ways than one, and I will bend over backwards so he never has any regrets.

One of the sacrifices he needed to make for us both was to have his facial features altered. The surgeon did an outstanding job, altering my man's face enough that he's no longer recognizable as *Elijah Ward*, but I miss the slightly bulbous tip his nose used to have. Still, if he was to start a new life as Elijah Reed, the intervention was necessary. A year on, he is fully healed, and I'd never be able to guess he's had anything done if I didn't know.

We frequently cook together too, and thanks to the nutritious meals and exercise outdoors he's also filled out and grew a bit sturdier, which makes him even less recognizable to the average onlooker.

"I'm sure the lenses will be fine." He kisses me in passing and rushes to the corridor to get snow boots on.

Even here, the Christmas spirit is overflowing. Eli has made enough colorful paper chains to drape them along every ceiling, so they're here too, next to crocheted stars, and wooden ornaments we've been painting since the end of the summer. There have been moments when I thought it would have been nice to switch to another activity, but when I look at what we've done with the place, all I feel is pride.

The weather on our private island can be harsh, so we have quite the collection of warm boots, coats, and more blankets than I can count. Eli's latest favorite is an electric blanket, for evenings when sitting by the fireplace isn't enough. Not that I mind. He can have everything he wants, for all I care, and yet he never abuses that privilege.

"I miss the silver," I say with a sigh, running my fingers through the dark blond waves that he grew out to shoulder-length.

He grins at me. "It is what it is if I'm to be undercover."

I sigh and kiss his lips. "I suppose we will need to wait until you're forty. Then, you can slowly stop dyeing it." I sit down to put on my own boots. "Excited?"

"You know I love this house. It's more than I could have dreamed of. When you said a house in Alaska, I imagined a cabin similar to the one we first hunkered down in, not an eco-mansion on a private island. *But I'm dying for this trip to town. And to a Christmas market too! I'm so excited."* Eli paces in place as he puts on his aviator hat trimmed with the fur of a rabbit I hunted myself.

"There's some people on the mainland who really want to meet my partner, but I'll make sure they don't overwhelm you," I joke, because while I have made some connections during the necessary trips off the island, I don't currently have any friends beyond Eli and our guard dogs.

With that, I zip myself up, put on a hat and grab his hand, leading the way outside.

Winter is harsh, even here in southern Alaska, but I'm happy to be far away from my former life, and this private paradise of ours is allowing that and more.

The island is big enough for me to hunt small animals and birds, which has become one of my main hobbies now that I'm no longer required to work, and I also often spend mornings fishing. Sometimes, we do little camping trips into the surrounding forest to make sure we're capable of surviving in the wild if push ever comes to shove. Still, our household wouldn't be complete without banana bread, candy, and large quantities of lube, so we can't quite live a self-sustainable lifestyle yet. But maybe in the future?

We did get into prepping a bit too much, but that's what happens when passionate people have lots of time on their hands. I wanted a secure house, so I ended up buying one with a bunker under it, which also leads to a secret passage out of the house through a tunnel. I, of course, hope we'll never have to use it, but it's better to be safe than sorry.

I did worry it would freak out Eli, but he got very excited about it, and while we often cook together, he's the one who does the canning, insisted on building a smokehouse for the fish, and keeps stock of our pantry. I wasn't sure how much we'd need, but after the harsh November we've had, I'm glad we had so many supplies.

The next layer of security is watching us with dark, attentive eyes.

"Good evening. You take good care of our home," I say to our German Shepherds and unlatch the door of their kennel. They're all big boys, and I make sure to give them all treats before we head down the path toward our private pier. The weather's great for this time of the year, so I'm not worried about taking Eli to shore on his very first outing since we arrived. Still, I'd rather he didn't get as seasick as he was on the journey we made from Washington state about a year ago.

"They're supposed to have pretzels," I say, grabbing Eli's hand to help him into the boat.

"I already love it! I made sure to stay hungry just so I can eat *everything*."

He doesn't know it yet, but in the evening I'll be taking him to a Christmas-themed feast in a private dining room at a local restaurant. The town is small, so it's not like Michelin star chefs are available, but the woman in charge of the place I'll be taking him to is an amazing cook and will dazzle Eli for sure.

"Bye home!" Eli waves at our house as he always does, and it's the most adorable little quirk that tells me how much he loves the place.

"It'll miss you too," I tell him and kiss his flushed cheek.

If you'd like to read to read a bonus scene, find the link at
http://kamerikan.com/freebies
We also have another dark Christmas book coming out this year <3
Check out Christmas Mafia Prince on Amazon
If you'd like to stay in touch, you can find us in our Facebook group, the Merikan Playroom.
Please, review this book on your favorite platform:)

CHRISTMAS MAFIA
Prince

K.A. MERIKAN

CHRISTMAS MAFIA PRINCE

K.A. MERIKAN

Expectations: Christmas break in Aspen.

Reality: Married to a mafia hitman who hunts people for sport.

Damen

All I want is to join my family for their annual Christmas hunt. But no, because that's apparently only for *married* men. Like I need a ring on my finger to shoot a man in the back.

Oh, yes, the tradition is hunting *people*. We keep some enemies alive and let them think they can escape. It's just a bit of festive fun, really, so it infuriates me that I, their best hitman, can't take part.

If my homophobic father thinks I'll marry a woman to qualify, he's delusional. This year, I'm coming home with a husband. And the perfect disaster of a man literally falls into my lap.

Green hair, tattoos, piercings, ripped jeans, and kohl-rimmed eyes. He's loud, drinks too much, and has no manners.

My father will *hate* him.

Killian

My type? Hot, toxic, and guaranteed to ruin my life. I've been cheated on, stalked, blackmailed, and I am *so* done. When my latest ex corners me at a bar with his signature mix of lies and threats, I ask a hot guy in a sharp suit to pretend he's my boyfriend.

He agrees, but asks me to be his fake husband at his family Christmas in return.

Free booze, a vacation in Aspen, and *drama*? Where do I sign up?

Only it turns out he's a mafioso, his family hunts people for sport, and if I don't play my cards right, I might end up on their trophy wall.

To survive the holidays, I just need to make sure I don't fall for my rich, gorgeous, and *psycho* fake husband. Easy-peasy.

Have I mentioned he's a millionaire, speaks French and f*cks like a demon?

"Christmas Mafia Prince" is a standalone **M/M dark romance** where a mafioso makes a stranger his fake husband for the holidays, but then falls for him hard and fast amidst a Christmas from hell adorned with mayhem, murder, and mistletoe.

Themes and tropes: abduction, fake relationship, wedding fever, fish out of water, opposites attract, cinderfella, size difference, hitman, possessive hero, dark humor, morally gray heroes, family drama, millionaire, my boyfriend is a killer!

AMAZON

VULTURE HOLLOW MC

CREEP

K.A. MERIKAN

CREEP

K.A. MERIKAN

He's my dream, my nightmare, my obsession.

Creep. Weirdo. Stalker. Monster under the bed.
Angel. Blond. Pillow Prince. Pisces.

Creep
They call me Creep and they're not wrong. I crawl under people's beds to feel close to them.

Tonight, my pick is a pretty blond twink with pink lips and blue eyes. My living fantasy. I meant to enjoy his company in secret, but I can't just lie there and listen when his boyfriend gets violent.

So I crawl out.

And I kill the bastard.

Now Angel's a witness to my crime, so... I take him.

I've never had a lover. Hell, I've never even kissed anyone. I'm twisted. Ugly. Unlovable.

But now that I've tasted Angel, I can't turn back. I need to make him mine.

Angel

I survived a string of shitty exes but didn't expect a monster in a leather jacket, with hair as black as night, to crawl out from under my bed and slaughter my abuser.

I fear the worst when he abducts me to his creepy den... but he doesn't hurt me. He's too shy to even speak to me when I'm awake and watches from the shadows instead.

It's when I pretend to sleep that he comes closer. The game makes it all the sweeter for him. When he reaches for me, he's careful but greedy, living out a fantasy he's too ashamed to ask for.

And I let him.

Because I'm curious. Because it makes my pulse spike. Because I'm starting to want it too.

"Creep" is a standalone, **M/M dark romance** where a lonely biker with an unusual kink abducts the object of his forbidden desire and finds salvation in the boy who should've run.

This is a book for readers who crave a protective monster with a broken past, twisted obsession, and the kind of love that crawls out from under your bed and refuses to let go.

If you're drawn to morally gray men, emotional tension, and the thrill of surrendering to danger... this one's for you.

AMAZON

ABOUT THE AUTHOR

K.A. MERIKAN IS A duo of queer writers who don't believe in following the well-trodden path. In their books you can dip your toe into dangerous romance with mafiosi, outlaw bikers and bad boys, all from the safety of your sofa. They love the weird and wonderful, stepping out of the box, and bending stereotypes both in life and in fiction. Their stories don't shy away from exploring the darker side of M/M romance, and feature a variety of anti-heroes, rebels, misfits, and underdogs who go against the grain.

Be prepared for shocking twists, dark humor, raw emotions, and sizzling hot scenes.

e-mail: **kamerikan@gmail.com**
http://kamerikan.com

More information about works in progress and publishing at:

Facebook: https://www.facebook.com/groups/1817541075240882

Patreon: https://www.patreon.com/kamerikan